Blind Sunday

Jessica Evans

SCHOLASTIC BOOK SERVICES

New York Toronto London Auckland Sydney Tokyo

Cover Photo by Owen Brown

ISBN 0-590-32155-2

12 11 10 9 8 7 6 5 4 3 2   .2 3 4 5 6/8

Printed in the U.S.A.   06

Blind
Sunday

A Wishing Star Book

I see beyond the range of sight
Henry David Thoreau

CHAPTER 1

Jeff was terribly, in fact, horribly shy. It was the thing that made him a loner; he looked normal enough, and he was reasonably good at most things, except conversation. The sports he went in for were the kind you could do on your own: swimming, and running, and long walks or bike rides. He was tall enough to have gone out for basketball. But nobody ever knew how good he was at that, because when it came time to try out for the team, he took one look at all the guys joshing around in the gym, waiting for the coach, and he knew that he'd be lousy at the jokes and towel-slapping and general team stuff that seemed to come so naturally to everyone but him. So he'd gone back home and worked off his anger at himself by shooting twenty-six baskets in a row against the backboard on the side of his garage, where no one could even see it.

It was stupid, but there it was. His mother kept telling him he'd grow out of it. His dad tried to give him man-to-man pep talks, but he wasn't much help, either. When Jeff asked what people talked about, his dad just said, "Oh, anything. It doesn't matter. Just anything."

Big help.

Well, he was used to it. Fifteen years of being a loner and he'd learned one thing: he might as well get used to it because he'd probably never learn to make small talk with anyone as long as he lived. He went his own way, got along just fine as long as a smile would do in place of a snappy remark.

Some of the girls at his school had tried to interest him, but so far he'd never even had a date. The thought of spending a whole evening, or even an afternoon, even an hour after school, trying to think of something to say to a girl made his mouth so dry he could hardly swallow. He figured he wouldn't mind so much once high school was over and he went to college. Then he could concentrate on learning to be an engineer, and the social thing wouldn't be such a problem. Engineers could spend all their time working over drafting boards and didn't have to yak with anyone if they didn't want to.

Sometimes he wondered whether being lonely kept on hurting all your life, or if you ever got used to it.

The municipal swimming pool wasn't too crowded on Saturday mornings if you got there early. There were a few kids from his school, in clusters, naturally; some other high-school types from across town; and a few older people getting their weekly exercise. The big gung-ho team types were all out on the practice fields, slapping each other on the back and snickering about the dates they'd had the night before. It was pretty peaceful at the huge indoor pool.

Jeff came out of the dressing room, tossed his robe and towel on a bench, and went right to the high board. He took off with a mediocre jackknife, cut the water cleanly and came up unexpectedly close to a pretty girl in a blue one-piece bathing suit. She was holding lightly to the rail at the pool's edge.

He shook the water from his head and was about to glide away when she startled him with a smile and a compliment.

"Neat dive," she said.

"Thanks," he mumbled. He could feel his cheeks turning red, and hoped she'd think it was just the effort of the dive. He hesitated, and decided he'd better just swim away, like a fish, because there was no way he was going to be able to think of anything to say to her. She was nice looking. Her wet hair clung to the contours of her face; her skin was fresh-looking and her eyes were kind of misty, soft and blue.

3

"What'd you call that dive?" she asked him.

She was smiling and her mouth was very round and red without the benefit of any lipstick or anything. She seemed very peaceful, not about to make some comment he couldn't answer.

"Jackknife," he said.

"Oh, that's right," she said laughing, but at herself, not at him. "Can you do a half-gainer?"

He was treading water and felt kind of clumsy, but she didn't seem to notice. She was looking at him with real interest and a pleasant smile on her face, and he wasn't blushing any more. He answered her rather easily.

"No, that's out of my class," he admitted.

"Oh."

There it was, the hideous, awful silence. Here was the inevitable moment when he should have had some witty, hilarious, wonderful, clever thing to say, and all he could think of was — nothing. He nodded at her, half-smiled, and awkwardly began to move away in the water. He swam past her and climbed up to the edge of the pool just beyond where she was hanging on. He grabbed his towel and busied himself drying his back and legs, not looking at her.

Out of the corner of his eye, he saw her gliding along the edge toward where he stood.

Her hands sort of walked along the rail and then gripped the side, and she pushed herself up out of the water neatly. She sat down on the edge with her legs dangling. She was right in front of him, but she wasn't looking at him, and he pretended not to see her, either.

But she knew he was there, all right. Her head half-turned in his direction, and she said clearly, "I'm Eileen."

He stopped drying himself and waited, not knowing what she wanted, and then he realized she was waiting for his name.

"Uh, I'm Jeff," he mumbled.

She laughed again. It was a nice laugh, though, and she said quickly, "You Tarzan, me Jane!"

Jeff smiled, and blushed. Now what was he supposed to say . . . he could hardly dive back into the pool and go off by himself. This girl — Eileen — obviously wanted to have a conversation with him, just one of those ordinary, pleasant, social, easy-going chats that people have all the time. Boy, did she ever pick herself a wrong one for that.

He stood there, wishing he were at the bottom of the pool, nine feet under the silent, undemanding blanket of water.

"Where do you go to school, Jeff?" she was saying. She was still not looking directly at him, sitting on the edge and letting her feet splash lazily in the water. She was just carrying on the conversation as if it meant nothing at all to her.

"Western High," he answered.

"I go to Eastern," she said. "I guess that's why we never met before. Do you come here often?"

"Oh . . . sometimes." What a dumb thing to say. She probably realized by now that he was a very dull fellow. But oh, how he wished he could think of one question to ask her back. Just one. He wasn't really dull, or dumb, but there was no way she'd ever know that.

"Hi, Lee!"

He turned to see an older woman approaching them.

"How's the water today?" the woman asked. She was talking to Eileen, who smiled up at her.

"Oh, hi, Mrs. Hays! The water is great, warmer than last week. Mrs. Hays, this is Jeff. He goes to Western. Jeff, this is Mrs. Hays. She's the librarian at my school, and my friend."

"Hi," Jeff said, blushing.

"Hello, Jeff," she answered pleasantly. "Well, that water does look inviting. Excuse me, I'm going to get my exercise for the day. Nice to meet you, Jeff."

She moved off toward the low diving board, and Jeff had to raise his voice to say, "Oh . . . same here, Mrs. Hays."

There was another silence. He watched the librarian climb the steps and dive into the water. Eileen didn't turn her head to follow her friend's movements; she seemed to be quite contented gazing off into space, sort of, and the silence didn't seem to bother her, either. Though you could never tell. He stood there, as usual, like a lump.

"Lee's my nickname," Eileen said.

That didn't seem to call for any real answer. He said nothing.

"Hey, you're the strong, silent type, huh?"

". . . I guess so . . . yeah. . . ." Desperately, he searched his mind. He thought of the doughnuts he had stashed in his robe pocket. ". . . Uh . . . want a doughnut?" he asked her.

Don't turn around and look at me, he glared silently at the back of her head. His face felt as red as the lettering on the towel.

"Sure!" she exclaimed. Her face lit up as she turned toward him, as if he'd offered her a diamond or something.

"Uh, just a minute. I'll go get them," he said, He nearly stumbled over his own feet as he took the few steps to the bench where he'd left his things, and he fumbled in the pocket of his robe. He was back at her side in a minute, with the two doughnuts held out on a piece of waxed paper. He sat down next to her on the edge of the pool.

"I've got two here," he said, holding them out for her to see. "Which do you want?"

"I don't care," she said, grinning, not looking at them.

"Take your pick," he urged her. He held them out in front of them. She reached out her hand, tentatively, but she was inches away from the offering. Her slim fingers flickered like antennae in the air.

Shocked, Jeff stared at her. Her eyes were clear, but they saw nothing.

Slowly, he moved the paper with the doughnuts directly under her fingers.

"Here," he said softly.

Her hand touched the fat one with sticky sugar all over it.

"Jelly," she said. "Right?"

"Yeah," he answered, staring at her.

She moved her fingers lightly to touch the other doughnut. "Uh . . . chocolate," she said. "My favorite." She picked it up and bit into it. "Ummmm," she said, "terrific!"

Jeff sat there, almost paralyzed, the paper with the jelly doughnut still in his outstretched hand, watching her. She laughed, suddenly, and the chocolate danced on her lips and dribbled down a bit on her chin. She lifted her hand to wipe her mouth before she spoke again.

"What's the matter?" she asked him. Her blind eyes were crinkled with amusement, and even though this time it was at his expense, he took no offense when she laughed. "Didn't you ever eat doughnuts with a blind girl before?"

He felt all confused and pained inside. He couldn't think of anything to say, but for once his concern was not with his own embarrassment, but with the feeling she must be having.

"Hey, are you okay?" she asked him.

"Uh . . . yeah," he managed to murmur.

"Well, relax, Jeff. It's okay!" Her hand reached out to the other doughnut, and she took it from his hand and lifted it toward his mouth. "Here," she said cheerfully.

He took it from her, and bit into it. They chewed in silence for a moment, but somehow it wasn't so awkward this time.

"Okay," she said after a moment, "now wipe that sugar mustache off your lip!"

He touched his upper lip, and, of course, she was right. There was a line of gooey sugar stuck there. He wiped it with the back of his hand.

"Okay?" she asked, with the smile he liked. It was the kind of smile that wanted to turn into a laugh any minute. It was a nice smile and a happy laugh, not the other kind. He found himself smiling, too. How did she know that he had sugar on his lip? She was funny, and nice.

9

"Hey, would you hold this a minute?" she asked him suddenly, handing him the uneaten half of her chocolate doughnut. He took it, not knowing what to expect.

"I feel a half-gainer coming on," she said, and sprang up to her feet. She walked slowly along the damp tiles toward the low diving board, touched its rails with her fingers and kept on going. She reached the ladder of the high board, and slowly, one foot at a time, began to climb up.

Jeff watched her, not realizing he was holding his breath. He saw the lifeguard, suddenly attentive, watching too, and he looked for Mrs. Hays, who was in the water. Her eyes were on Eileen, too, as she slowly ascended the ladder. Mrs. Hays was smiling.

Eileen reached the high board. She took five measured steps to the edge. Her toes felt for the end of the board, and then she turned around to count back the two steps she would need for the spring. She waited, poised there.

"Okay, Lee, it's clear!" Mrs. Hays called out, and Eileen smiled, took a deep breath, and sprang off the board in a very graceful half-gainer.

She broke from the water with ease and swam back toward the edge where Jeff was sitting.

"Like it?" she asked, laughing up at him.

"Wow! That was great! Really!" he answered with complete sincerity.

Her long, shining hair plastered around her head like a cap, her clear blue eyes laughing up at him, she opened her mouth like a little fish, and moved her arms in easy, effortless strokes to stay afloat.

"Hey, what are you waiting for?" she asked him.

"Huh?"

"I need my half a chocolate doughnut!" she said. He reached down with it, and held it to her mouth. She took a big bite and chewed it with enjoyment. He took a bite of his, too, and for no reason at all they were both laughing.

"Hi, Lee!"

"Hi, Marge! Hey, Marge, this is my friend Jeff. He goes to Western. Jeff, meet Marge."

"Hi."

"Hi."

"That was a nice dive, Lee."

"Thanks. I get my energy from chocolate doughnuts."

In the presence of the long-haired blonde girl, Jeff found himself tongue-tied again, as usual. She had looked at him only briefly, and acknowledged the introduction without smiling. Suddenly he felt like an intruder.

"Going home soon, Lee?" Marge said, ignoring him. "I've got to leave right this minute or my mother will have a fit. We could go back together, unless you're staying around?"

There was a very brief pause, not even

noticeable, really. It was not until hours later that Jeff realized maybe Eileen had been waiting for him to say something. But of course he didn't, and after a moment she nodded and pulled herself out of the pool.

"Well . . . bye, Jeff. It was nice meeting you. And thanks a lot for the doughnut. Saved my life!" she said.

"Uh . . . oh, sure. That's okay. Nice meeting you."

"Well . . . bye, then."

"Bye."

The two girls headed for the dressing room, and Jeff was left holding the paper with two ends of doughnuts on it. He crumpled them up and tossed them in the refuse can. Then he climbed the ladder to the high board and tried his jackknife again. Maybe she'd teach him the half-gainer, if he ever got up the nerve to ask her. Why hadn't he thought of that when she was sitting right there with him?

He dove down almost to the bottom of the pool and swam around underwater until his breath gave out. People's legs looked weird underwater. He turned and ducked to avoid them. Then, as he broke the surface and shook the water out of his eyes, it occurred to him to wonder what it must be like to see nothing, nothing at all, ever. He'd never thought about that before. Too bad, she was really pretty, too. And not too hard to talk to, not so hard as most girls. Too bad she was blind; something might have come of it. There was the big dance coming up, the cooperative after the East-West game. If she weren't blind, maybe he would have got up the nerve between now and the dance to ask her. But blind girls probably don't dance, and anyway, who was he kidding? If she could see anything, she'd probably be so popular she'd never have time for a lunk like him anyway. He climbed out of the pool and went to get dressed.

"Well, I guess you could say he was kind of good looking," Marge said in answer to Eileen's casual question, as they walked home.

"I don't know why I even asked," she said cheerfully. "I don't even know what 'kind of good looking' means."

"Well, he's tall, and dark, and he's got nice features, but he's awfully shy," Marge tried to explain.

"Well, I know all that," Eileen said. "Except the part about his being dark, but I could have guessed that. I know he's tall and I know he's shy. What I asked was whether he was handsome. Not that it matters. How could it matter to me?" She laughed at her own question.

"Well, as a matter of fact, I think you make a very attractive couple," Marge said determinedly. "Really."

"We're hardly a couple," Eileen said. "I'll probably never see him again. I just wondered what he looked like, that's all."

CHAPTER 2

"Morning, Jeff."

The kitchen was strangely quiet, Jeff's father thought. The radio wasn't even on. He poured himself a cup of coffee and joined his son at the breakfast table.

He looked at Jeff's somber, thoughtful face, and waited for a "good morning" that didn't come. Jeff was deep in thought.

"Hey, Jeff . . . I'm really sorry about your pet rock dying. No wonder you're so depressed," he said.

Jeff looked up from his uneaten cereal, startled. He had been so deep in his own thoughts he hadn't even noticed his father coming into the room. He grinned sheepishly.

"Sorry, Dad. Good morning."

"What's wrong, son?"

His father was a nice man, concerned and loving. They just didn't seem to reach each other with words any more. Jeff remembered how easy it used to be; his dad seemed to know all the answers to everything, but that was when Jeff was a little kid. Lately, the answers had been no help at all. He knew it was because the questions were more complicated, and he wasn't even able to think of the right words for asking them sometimes. Sometimes he didn't even know for sure what questions he needed to ask; how could he expect his dad or anyone else in the whole world to be able to answer questions when he didn't even know how to ask them.

His dad was sipping the coffee, and watching him over the rim of the cup, waiting with his kind eyes, wanting to help.

"Dad . . . how do you talk to someone?"

His father set the cup down carefully. His face showed his concern, his real caring, and it showed his confusion, too. Jeff knew at once that he hadn't put it right, somehow, and that his dad wasn't going to be able to help.

"Talk to someone?" he repeated.

"Yeah. . . . How do you make conversation? Like . . . when you just want to be friendly, you know?"

His dad still looked puzzled, as if Jeff had been speaking some foreign language. But he didn't know how else to put it.

"People seem to talk to each other all the time, and I just can't. I mean, I can never think of anything to say. I want to be friendly, you know, when I meet somebody, or even with someone I know from my class . . . but I get all tongue-tied."

"You mean small talk?" his father asked.

"Yeah, that's it. Small talk. I mean, how do you think of things to say?"

His father's forehead creased with two deep lines as he thought it over, and then he said in a gentle voice, "Maybe you try too hard, Jeff."

"Well, it's supposed to be relaxed, right? Fun? I mean, people talk to each other and they smile and laugh and it doesn't mean anything, except that they're being friendly. Well, what do they say? That's what I can never think of. . . ." He stopped. His dad had obviously never had the problem, himself, or if he ever did he'd forgotten what it was like and how to solve it. He was one of those people who just *knew*.

"Well," his dad said finally, "the first thing you should believe is that everything you say doesn't have to be brilliant . . . or funny. Just relax and be yourself."

"Myself! Myself is tongue-tied. Nothing comes out. I'm lousy at it, that's what being myself is, so when somebody is friendly to me, I stand there like a dumb jerk."

"Oh, come on, Jeff. You're being awfully hard on yourself, aren't you? You're bright and you're interested in lots of things. It's just a temporary phase, you'll see."

Jeff was silent.

"Jeff?"

Those kind eyes were waiting for him to say something. In a sudden, desperate burst of words, Jeff let it all out.

"There's this girl I met yesterday at the pool, and . . . well, she talked to me, and was really nice, and friendly, and I couldn't think of anything to say. Dad, did you ever know a blind person?"

His father had been sipping at his coffee. He set the cup back down in the saucer carefully. He frowned at Jeff.

"Is that your idea of small talk?" he asked with a wry groan.

"No . . . but . . . this girl I met. . . . Well, she's blind. I didn't even know it, at first. She's really pretty and very nice, laughs a lot and makes jokes and all . . . and I couldn't even talk to her."

"Because she's blind?"

"No! I couldn't think of anything to say, not anything . . . before I even noticed that she couldn't see."

"Well, was it easier to talk to her after you found out that she couldn't see?"

"Well, that didn't seem to make any difference. I mean . . . I don't know. Anyway, I'll probably never see her again anyway."

His father caught his glance, and they looked across the chasm of the breakfast table at each other for a long minute. Then his dad said, "But you'd like to see her again? Is that it?"

"Well . . . I don't know. She was nice and all, but that's just the problem, Dad. If I called her up, or went over to her school someday to meet her . . . what would I say?"

"You might start off with . . . let's see . . . 'Hi, I'm Jeff, remember me, we met at the pool.' How's that for openers?"

"Yeah, and then what?"

"Well, that depends on what she says. One thing leads to another."

"Everybody else seems to do it so well, no problem at all. For instance, there's this dance coming up, and all the guys are lining up dates and they're all finding it so easy."

"I doubt it. Maybe it just looks that way to you. I can guarantee you're not the only young man your age who has trouble talking to girls."

"Maybe so, but nobody admits it. Maybe I'm just the only one who admits it."

"What about this dance that's coming up?"

"Oh, it's just a dance, nothing special . . . between the two schools, after the game two weeks from now."

"And you'd like to go?"

"Well . . . yeah, I would. But if I did, what

19

would I talk about? To a girl, for the whole evening?"

"You want to ask this blind girl to be your date?"

"No! I mean, I don't even know her. I only saw her that once, yesterday. She probably thinks I'm really stupid."

"Jeff, is that really why you don't want to ask her?"

Jeff was puzzled. "Why, sure. What other reason is there? That's what I've been trying to tell you. I just wouldn't know what to say to her."

"Oh. You know, sometimes it seems like you're trying to tell me something more than you're actually saying, Jeff. It's hard to follow you, sometimes. You talk about not having any small talk, and about this pretty girl who's blind, and about the dance. I thought maybe you were trying to tell me that you wanted to invite this girl to the dance."

"Well, just supposing I did. I've still got the problem of how to talk to her."

His father had finished his coffee, and now he rose from the table. He put his hand on Jeff's shoulder for a minute.

"Just be yourself, Jeff," he said, and then he went out through the kitchen and down the stairs to his workroom.

It sounded like a cop-out to Jeff. He had the feeling that he and his father had been right on the edge of something, and then his dad backed away from it. Sighing, he cleared the plates so his mother wouldn't have to face the Sunday morning clutter when she came down for her breakfast later. He went up to put on his track shoes and headed out to the park. Three times around the zoo was seven miles. Maybe the run would clear his head.

He saw her from a distance in the park. She was with two other girls and had her hands lightly through their arms. They were laughing and strolling near the elephants. He just kept on running.

"Well, I think it's just stupid," Pam was saying. "All that money for decorations." She half leaned across Eileen to direct her words at Marge as they walked along in the sunshine.

"I don't," Marge retorted. "How often do we have a dance with Western? Once a year!"

"So?" Pam shrugged. She tossed a peanut to the smallest elephant, who caught it easily in his trunk and popped it into his mouth.

"So, it should look nice," Marge said.

The three girls ambled toward the bear cages.

"But we could hire a better group with that money," Pam pointed out. "Music is more important than all that tacky crepe paper and stuff." She felt strongly about it, and looked to Eileen for support. "What do you think, Lee?"

Eileen smiled. "I agree," she said thoughtfully. "But then . . . I'm hardly the one to judge decorations."

She giggled, and felt the quick relief of sensing that Pam and Marge were smiling, too, in response to her joking. It was a trick she'd learned long ago to put people at their ease so they might forget for a moment, anyway, that she was different. Then they wouldn't get all tense and hung up in the middle of a conversation. She was relieved when Pam and Marge went right on with their argument.

"When I go to a dance, I like to dance," Pam said firmly. "Not look at decorations. And so does Mark. He said so."

"Mark!" Eileen put in. "You've got a date with Mark? He finally asked you?"

"Yes," Pam said. She squeezed her friend's arm with her own pleasure. "He asked me last night. He called me on the phone and talked for hours before he finally got around to asking."

"Oh, wow!" Marge exclaimed. "That's great, Pam! I'm going with Erik. Of course. Why don't we double?"

"Why don't we triple?" Eileen laughed. "I have a date with Robert Redford."

Oh, oh, that was going too far. She felt them tense up, and knew that a look had passed over her between the other two girls. A look of chagrin and worse . . . pity. The thing she hated most. When would she learn how far she could go in her jokes about herself, without making other people self-conscious?

"Why the sudden morbid silence?" she said hurriedly, still smiling, trying to put her friends at ease again. "Don't you believe me?"

"Ah, Lee, come on . . . don't joke," Pam said miserably.

"Hey, listen, why not? What are we supposed to do, ignore the fact that I don't have a date? Or cry about it? Hey, you guys aren't going to start feeling sorry for me, I hope," she said quickly. "Come on," she said, "I think I smell hot dogs, am I right? I'm starved."

"Me, too," Marge said quickly, and Pam led the way to the man with the umbrella stand just off the path that led between the animals and the joggers running ceaselessly around the perimeter of the park.

"Hey, isn't that Erik?" Pam said suddenly, as they were sitting down on a bench to have their snack.

"Where? Oh, yes!" Marge said, with sudden animation. "Doesn't he look cute in his running shorts? Look at those muscles in his legs. Oops, there he goes. Bye, Erik."

They all laughed, and concentrated on juggling the franks and soda cans.

"I guess we can compromise on the decorations a little bit," Marge decided, thinking out loud, "if we can come up with something really clever."

"And cheap," Pam agreed.

"What are you going to wear?"

Eileen sensed that look again, passing between her friends on either side of her.

"If I were going," she said cheerfully, "I'd get a red dress, the brightest red color I could find, so nobody would notice the cheap decorations," she laughed and was rewarded by the spontaneous giggles of her friends once again. But she was wondering, secretly . . . what was it like, to see bright colors?

"Lee is right," Marge said. "The music's the thing. Let's spend the whole budget on the group, and anybody who thinks the aud looks cruddy without crepe paper can just go mope in a corner."

"I hear the birds chirping over there," Eileen said. "Want to walk over that way?"

She crumpled up the napkin in her hand with the empty soda can, and held out her hand to take the empties from Pam and Marge. They handed her their litter without much thought. Carefully, Eileen got up from the bench and moved along the sidewalk path to the large refuse can she knew was six paces away. She dumped the stuff inside and turned to her friends, waiting for them to join her. They linked arms again, and strolled toward the huge cage where the colorful birds were anticipating their feeding time. Everyone around the area admired the brilliant reds and greens and blues of the squawking, fluttering, soaring, diving birds. Eileen listened with rapt pleasure to their various and fascinating music.

CHAPTER 3

Eileen had learned to read and write Braille when she was in the first grade. Her teacher was Mrs. Hays, who still worked half her time at the special school for the blind and the other half as the librarian of Eastern High. Eileen felt incredibly lucky to have her friend and mentor right there in her own school, and the library was one of her favorite places to be. Not that she was a bookworm or any kind of scholar; actually, she'd much rather be out in the park on sunny days, or at the ball games or the pool . . . like anybody else. She *was* like anybody else. Exactly. Normal, the right size and shape for a fifteen-year-old girl and no brighter or dumber than most. Her interests were exactly like Pam's and Marge's and all the other kids; people told her she was more cheerful than most, but she had to be, to keep everybody from getting uptight around her. People really reacted strangely to being around a blind girl; she was used to it, but she'd never, never understand it. What was the big deal? She wasn't any kind of freak or anything. Sometimes she wondered if she looked different from other people. Maybe she was grotesquely ugly or something, but there was no way for her to know that. Maybe people were lying when they told her she was pretty. Oh well, she couldn't let that matter. Much.

Her parents were terrific, but prejudiced, of course. Naturally they thought she was pretty, but she'd heard or read someplace that parents were blind when it came to their children. The main thing was that they treated her exactly the way they treated her older sister. They *expected* her to be normal, and didn't make a big thing of it when she managed to tie her own shoes or find her way out of her bed in the morning. She had her jobs to do around the house, like her sister did, and she hadn't even known she was different at all until she started going to the regular public school.

Mrs. Hays had helped, so much. Besides teaching Eileen to read Braille, she answered her millions of questions about the things she found out about for the first time in books. Things like colors, and how high the sky was overhead, and what different clouds were, and what it meant for things to look a certain way.

Besides being a super teacher, Mrs. Hays was the one who insisted that Eileen face the fact that she *was* different from sighted people. First, she helped her to a "normal" life, and second, she made Eileen realize that a truly normal life was not quite possible. Ever. It was, in fact, a very important and difficult thing to accept, but she was learning, thanks to Mrs. Hays. She fought it, but they both knew that she was getting mature enough to accept her limitations, too.

She was writing her paper for history class in the library on Monday, quickly punching out the Braille symbols with her stylus and tape, checking facts and footnotes in the cumbersome volumes spread out before her on the table. The library was humming as it always did, with the rustle of book pages, restlessly twisting students who'd rather be outdoors, an occasional whisper and the sound of chairs being pulled out, footsteps going past. It was comforting, and familiar, but Eileen longed to be out of there as the others did. She wondered if Pam and Marge were almost finished with their papers; they were sitting across from her, and she heard their pens scratching as they wrote.

A problem. She puzzled over a word, and finally got up from her seat and went quietly over to Mrs. Hays' desk.

"How do you spell 'correspondence'?" she asked softly.

"With an 'e-n-c-e,' " Mrs. Hays answered.

"Thanks," Eileen said. She punched in the word on the tape. She handed it to Mrs. Hays. "Here," she said. "What do you think?"

Mrs. Hays ran her fingers over the tape quickly to read it, while Eileen stood before her, shifting her weight from one foot to the other. "Ummmm . . . not bad . . . oh, here, Abigail Adams . . . there's no 'e' in Abigail," she said.

"Okay, I'll fix it," Eileen sighed.

Still reading with her deft fingers, Mrs. Hays commented again. "Oh-oh . . ."

"Now what?" Eileen asked.

"Correspondence."

"I used an 'e' like you said."

"No, that's okay," Mrs. Hays said slowly, "the spelling's right. But you used the long form — fourteen letters. You should have used the Braille contractions for 'ence'. It would have saved you four letters."

Eileen frowned, just a shadow passing over her face, gone as quickly as she could control it. She hoped Mrs. Hays had not seen; she didn't want to seem ungrateful, sullen. It was a drag, though, when someone you really trusted had a lapse of understanding.

"I like to spell it the long way," she said quietly. "That's how it's *spelled*."

"Not in Braille," Mrs. Hays said firmly. "In Braille, it's only eleven letters."

"Braille is for blind people," Eileen snapped,

29

but she smiled as she said it. Her smile was her defense, her armor, and her way of showing that she didn't mind. Not at all. And hoped other people wouldn't, either.

"Lee," Mrs. Hays said kindly, "it's faster."

"So, what's the hurry?" Eileen said, trying to laugh.

Mrs. Hays held out her hand to Eileen, and with a barely perceptible touch, indicated that she should sit down next to the librarian's desk. Eileen slid reluctantly into the chair, ready for the lecture, hating it, knowing Mrs. Hays was right about these things, but hating to have to face it all the time.

"Look, Lee, I know you want to be just like everybody else, I know how important it is to you, even in spelling; but the truth is, you're not."

Lee started fumbling with her hands, groping across Mrs. Hays' desk awkwardly. She pushed papers aside and nearly knocked over the little vase of flowers she knew always stood near the corner. She caught it, but kept on slapping her open hands around as if feeling wildly for something.

"What are you looking for?" Mrs. Hays said, peering suspiciously at Eileen's antics.

"My tin cup and pencils," Eileen said, half laughing and half trying not to cry.

"Oh, come on, Lee, you know what I mean. We've talked about it so many times, haven't we? And I know you hate it, but you agreed, didn't you, that it's better to face facts in the long run? Come on, now."

"Won't you help a poor blind girl out?" Eileen retorted, still reaching with her open hands into the air above Mrs. Hays' papers. She clutched at an imaginary handout, and smiled her most pathetic little grin. "Oh, thank you, sir," she mocked.

"Oh, Lee! Be serious. Sometimes you carry this independence thing too far, you know you do," Mrs. Hays said. She reached out to touch Eileen's hand, but just then the bell rang, sounding through the school to signal the end of the study hour.

"Oops, got to go," Eileen said. She stood up. "Between classes is the best time for begging."

Mrs. Hays laughed. "You're a nut, do you know that?"

Gathering her books and papers, Eileen shrugged and grinned. "Sure I do," she said. They did understand each other. "See you later?" she asked casually.

"Can't today. I'm teaching an extra class at the Braille Institute. See you tomorrow," Mrs. Hays said.

Eileen hesitated for just a moment, while the rush of students leaving the library clattered around them. "Those blind kids are lucky to have you," she murmured. "Don't be too hard on 'em!"

"I wish they were all like you," her friend

said in a quiet voice. "Go on, now, you'll be late for class."

Eileen didn't need her cane in school. She could find her way out of the library without even having to feel for the card files, the shelves along the wall leading to the door. Out in the hall, she counted paces to the stairway, and joined the crowds heading for the classrooms on the third floor.

"Hi, Lee!" a girl's voice sang out near her, and she turned with a smile of greeting. Her friend Ellie took her arm easily and they walked down the hall to history class together. She had lots of friends, just like everyone else. Girlfriends, anyhow. The boys were nice enough to her, but no one had ever asked her out on a date.

Resolutely, she turned her thoughts to Abigail Adams and *her* problems. She took her seat in the classroom and tried not to listen to the chatter all around her before the teacher took over. It seemed as if no one could talk of anything these days except that dance two weeks away.

In another classroom on the other side of the city, Jeff sat daydreaming while his math teacher droned on and on about the problem she had outlined on the blackboard.

"So bY and cZ times xN and $4Qe$ equals. . . ."

How did blind people manage in school if they couldn't see the blackboard, or the maps, or even other kids' faces?

". . . 6dg plus 4n over x . . ."

What was it like to be really so different from everyone else . . . but that girl, Eileen, had seemed normal at first, until he realized that she couldn't see. What was it like to be the object of people's pity? Did anyone laugh at her? Kids could be hideously cruel, sometimes. What did she think, inside her head, about . . . about everything?

"Therefore, the value of 'y' is . . . what? Hands, please?"

He supposed they had lots of books in Braille, and cassettes and records to listen to, but still, it must be a lot harder to learn stuff that way. How did she manage to be so *cheerful*?

"Jeff?"

Maybe she had been extra nice to him — and she really had been nicer than any other girl he'd ever tried to talk with — because she wasn't able to see how he blushed and shriveled when someone tried to make conversation. Maybe they were both freaks, and she had some kind of extra-sensory thing to compensate for her blindness that made her pick him out.

"Jeff!"

"Ma'am?" He was startled. In the silence

around him he realized that the teacher had called his name several times, and everyone in the class was looking at him and waiting, smiling and ready to laugh at him.

"What is the value of 'Y'?" she repeated. She had moved up the aisle and was standing right over him, deliberately making him the center of attention. Punishment for having his thoughts elsewhere; he deserved it. Blushing furiously, he muttered a helpless attempt at polite response.

"Uh . . . I'm here, Miss Curry."

"Well, then?"

She waited. Everyone waited, ready to snicker. Jeff stared straight ahead at the blackboard and went over the equation with calculator-like efficiency in his head.

"Uh . . . the value of 'Y' is . . . db7. . . ." he said, almost whispering.

Miss Curry looked almost disappointed, but had the grace to laugh, and the echoing laughter of his classmates was more like a sigh of relief than a jibe at him.

"Good," Miss Curry said curtly. "Go back to sleep," she added, as she moved toward the front of the room again, drawing the attention of the class with her.

Jeff's blood slowly returned to circulate through the rest of his body, leaving his face almost normal. He felt like a real jerk, but that wasn't news. When the bell rang, the other kids dived out of the room and he followed, alone as usual.

On an impulse he didn't try to analyze, he took a bus ride over to the east side of town. He alighted at the stop near Eastern High, and saw the kids strolling out in pairs and small groups. The big rush was over, and he supposed he'd missed her. Why would a blind girl hang around after school, anyway? She could hardly participate in any of the activities, like band or orchestra, or even chorus, or work on the newspaper . . . could she? Well, maybe she took extra time in the library or something. He'd just sort of mosey over, stay on the opposite side of the street and watch the trickle of students from the school as they dispersed in all directions. No reason, just some kind of curiosity. He wouldn't know what to say to her if he did see her, anyway. And she couldn't see him, so he was safe enough just not doing anything, just standing there. He had nothing better to do.

Then he saw her, coming down the wide steps of the school with her friend he had met at the pool, Marge Something. She wasn't nearly as pretty as Eileen, although she had long, straight blonde hair that she kept tossing a lot. She seemed to be looking for someone over her shoulder, while she casually guided Eileen down the steps and kept up some kind of chatter. He leaned against a big old tree on the other side of the street. He couldn't tell what they were yammering about, but he could see that Marge was peering around in search of someone— oh, there he was! A lean, super-muscled guy with a football sweater on strolled over to the two girls, and Marge suddenly became all smiles.

Jeff couldn't hear the conversation, of course, but he saw the result of it and he was hit with a sudden, terrible pain inside, worse even than his own embarrassment in math class. In his fertile imagination, he could reconstruct the whole scene; it was almost as if he had extra-sensitive hearing.

The jock sidled up to the two girls and they exchanged "hi's."

"Oh, hi, Erik," Marge said, as if surprised to see him, as he matched his steps to theirs.

"Hi, Marge. Hi, Eileen."

"Hi, Erik." Eileen's smile was really special, even from here it lighted up her whole face. The three of them ambled slowly down the wide walkway from the school to the street.

"So . . . how'd it go?" Erik asked.

"Awful!" Marge replied, with the kind of animated enthusiasm that ought to be reserved for reporting airline disasters. "I had this terrible French test. . . ."

"Yeah?" Erik answered, as if eager for all the gory details.

"If I make a D, I'm lucky," she giggled.

36

"Yeah . . . I know just how you feel," he said.

The three of them reached the sidewalk and the two girls started to turn to the left. But Erik tapped Marge on the shoulder, lightly, indicating that she should stop. He gestured toward some other kids who were hanging around the monument on their right.

"I got a Spanish mid-term tomorrow," he was saying, but his hands were pantomiming something else. He pointed to the right and it was crystal clear that he meant for Marge to ditch Eileen and join the others with him.

Marge shook her head "no" and frowned slightly, but her voice was still shrill and lively as she went on talking for Eileen's benefit. Jeff could hear every word now, as they stood at the edge of the street.

"Oh, gee," Marge said, "I guess you'll have to hit the books tonight, then. Mid-terms already!" She was shaking her head at him as she and Eileen stood arm-in-arm, supposedly saying good-bye to him. But their private conversation was very much alive.

Erik was waving both his hands in the air, insisting with obvious gestures that Marge come with him. He stood only a couple of feet away, and Jeff couldn't help wondering how Eileen could be missing all this pantomime. Even if she couldn't actually see it.

"Yeah," Erik was saying, "and there's this great movie on TV, too."

"I guess you'll have to miss it," Marge said. Her eyes were roving wildly from her boyfriend's pleading gestures to the group waiting at the statue. Someone waved to her and she bit her lip. She was weakening.

"Yeah . . . I hate to miss it, Bogart," Erik said. He jerked his head in a final invitation, with a questioning look at her, and Eileen's "loyal" friend suddenly nodded her head in one short movement. Yes.

"Too bad," Erik said, grinning. And then he winked at Marge broadly. "Well," he said, "see you!"

"Yeah," Marge answered. "Okay. Bye, Erik. See you!"

"So long, Erik," Eileen chimed in. "See you."

"Sure, right. Bye, Eileen."

Jeff thought about that, Eileen saying "see you." It tugged at him strangely, even through his disgust at the behavior of her so-called friends. He watched Erik sauntering off toward the monument, as Marge and Eileen turned in the other direction and walked a couple of steps. He knew what was going to happen, and he felt so sorry for Eileen that for the first time in his life he felt like punching somebody. But he stood, as usual, mute and paralyzed, watching and listening while it happened.

Marge stopped in her tracks, and Eileen stopped too.

"Oh, gee!" Marge said, as if she'd just thought of something.

"What's the matter?"

"I have to go back. I forgot something."

"Oh. Okay, I'll wait here," Eileen said.

"Uh . . . no . . . no . . . I'll be a while," Marge stammered awkwardly. She turned her head to look at the kids waiting for her, and then she said quickly, too quickly, "I've got to find something. You'd better not wait, really."

Eileen's hand dropped from its light hold through Marge's arm. Her smile never wavered as she said, "Hey, listen, Marge, if you want to go off with Erik, it's okay with me."

Shocked, guilty, Marge shifted her weight uncomfortably from one foot to the other. "Huh?" was all she managed to say.

Sunnily, evenly, Eileen said, "Don't you think I heard all that "signing" going on? Like, he did everything except send out smoke signals."

"What do you mean, Lee?" asked Marge, looking like she was either going to cry or run away.

"Oh, Marge, I mean it's perfectly okay, if you two want to be alone. I know three's a crowd. Only . . . please . . . don't be hypocrites?"

Something made the kids hanging around the monument burst out into hilarity. Jeff was pleased to see that Marge was feeling about as high as a squashed ant just then.

"Gee, Lee . . . I . . ." she stammered.

Eileen smiled at her, showing it was all right. "Go on," she said pleasantly. "I'll get home okay. I could do it in the dark!"

Erik was waving impatiently at Marge. Quickly, she said, "I'm sorry, Lee. I didn't mean anything. I truly am sorry."

"Sure, I know. See you in school tomorrow." Eileen reached out to touch Marge's arm, comforting her friend as if she were the one who'd been hurt. "Okay?" she said softly. "So long. Go on, better hurry. I can tell — Erik is getting impatient. Right?"

"Oh, Lee . . ."

"For heaven's sake, don't start feeling guilty about me! I'm fine. Go on, have a good time. See you tomorrow," Eileen said gaily.

Marge hesitated only a fraction of a second, and then turned and walked off quickly to join Erik and the others. Eileen stood alone, smiling still, and her clear blank eyes were filled with pain. But only for a brief, brief moment, and only Jeff was there to see. He watched her open her schoolbag and reach inside for something. It was a folded stick, which she snapped open in three places. A smooth narrow stick painted white, with a red tip and a strap to go around her wrist at the other end. She let the tip touch the pavement in front of her, and then gently began to sweep the stick back and forth in front of her as she walked.

Jeff watched her, not knowing what to do, what to think. Would she want his company? What could he say to her?

He watched her walking along at a normal pace, with the stick swinging carefully ahead of her. When she reached the corner, she stopped and waited. The light was green, but she didn't know that. She stood, waiting, smiling at no one and nothing in particular.

Before he thought about it, he had run across the street and was standing just behind her. The light had turned red.

CHAPTER 4

"Uh . . . hi."

She turned toward him, her unseeing eyes smiling now along with her mouth.

"Oh, hi!" she responded.

"Remember me?" he asked.

"Uh . . . I think so. Say some more," she said, laughing.

"Gee . . uh . . . what should I say? Uh . . . the light has changed. Can I help you across?"

Nicely, but firmly, she answered, "No! I can manage."

She crossed the street briskly, her stick easily swinging ahead of her, and Jeff followed close behind.

"You're at the curb," he said.

Eileen's stick touched the curb and she took the step easily, and then turned toward him with a mock-serious look on her face. "Now I know who you are," she said. "You're Fido, the guide dog."

Stung, his first instinct was to duck, to re-
treat, to get away from her. But at the same
instant he remembered the look of pain that
had crossed her face when her friend had
ditched her. She must take a lot, all the time,
and who was he to get his feelings hurt.
Anyway, she had a right to sock out at somebody, even if it was just an innocent eaves-
dropping bystander.

He didn't leave, but forced himself to walk
alongside her, thinking maybe she didn't want
him, but for once not running away from a
confrontation.

"I'm sorry," he said quietly.

She turned her cheerful smile to him as
they stood there on the corner. "You don't
have to apologize," she said. "*I* should. It's
just that I like to manage by myself. You're
the boy I met at the pool, right?"

"Yeah."

"You go to Western. . . ."

"Uh huh," he nodded, but aware that she
couldn't see his nod, he started trying desperately to think of something to say. Nothing
came to him.

It didn't seem to matter to her, if she noticed his problem at all. She went right on
talking as if he were holding up his end. "So,
what are you doing over on this side of town?"

"Uh . . . I had an errand to do."

"Oh. Well, it was nice seeing you," she

said. She tossed her head, clutched her books to herself with one hand, and with the other started moving her white stick in its rhythmic pattern, like radar ahead of her. She went a few steps before he found his tongue.

"My errand's done!" he shouted, and caught up with her a bit out of breath. He lowered his voice. "I . . . uh, I'm going this way."

"Okay," she said. She kept on walking.

"May I join you?"

"Sure," she laughed. "I mean, it seems you already have!"

They walked along the sidewalk for a little while, and Jeff found himself feeling much more at ease. He even thought of something to say.

"Hey . . . I'm kind of hungry. . . . How about a hamburger?"

She grinned and in that almost involuntary way that girls have, she hugged her books close to her. "Sure," she said happily, "that'd be nice!"

Jeff was enormously relieved. "Okay, let's go!"

"Do you know this part of town very well?" she asked him as they walked.

"No, not really."

"There's a place where all the kids go, just on the next block. Maybe you can see it from here. It's called The Joint."

"Oh, yeah," Jeff said, peering ahead. "The

place with the awning?" He stopped himself quickly; how could she know if there was an awning or not?

"That's The Joint," she nodded. "Want to go there? We don't have to. There are other places."

"No, no, that's okay. I mean, I don't mind. I mean, unless you'd rather?" Hopeless, he'd really muddled it this time. Maybe she didn't want to go where all the kids who knew her went, not with him, anyway. And how was he going to feel, walking into a place crowded with kids who all knew each other, and him with a blind girl none of them wanted to bother with? And what were they going to have to talk about for the time it took to get the burgers and eat them?

But in a moment, after crossing another street with Eileen in the lead, they came to the popular hangout called The Joint. He followed her right to the door.

"I always know when I'm in front of The Joint because of the awning," Eileen told him. "You can feel the change in temperature when the sun gets blocked out. Anyway, the kids make so much noise anybody could follow their ears right to the spot." She reached for the door and he wasn't quick enough to open it for her. He followed her inside. She hesitated, just a moment, inside the door, and he held out his arm automatically, without thinking. She reached for it easily, and he led them both to an empty booth.

He saw Marge and Erik there with the other kids who had been hanging around waiting for them. Even after they had passed them, he felt Marge staring at the back of his head, and wondered abruptly if Eileen felt it, too.

"Well," he said brightly, "here we are."

"Yes."

"Nice place," he said. He could feel his throat drying up again.

"Yes," she answered. She was still smiling, and it wasn't phony, either. He could see that now, as close as they were across the narrow little table. She really seemed to smile all the time because she was happy. Was that possible?

The silence was beginning to get awkward, but the waiter finally came over and put down two glasses of water. He did a little double-take when he saw Eileen's hand grope for it and move it carefully square in front of her. She must have sensed that, too, because she turned away, concentrating on her stick, which she folded up and stuck inside her bag.

"What'll you have?" the waiter asked Jeff.

"Uh, a burger and a chocolate malt," he answered.

"And what'll she have?"

Eileen flared in a quick burst of anger.

"*She* will have a cheeseburger, a vanilla shake, and french fries," she said icily.

The waiter shrugged, with an uncaring, mildly curious glance at Jeff, and walked away, muttering "Okay, okay."

"That makes me mad," Eileen said, calming as quickly as she had angered.

"I noticed," Jeff said.

"Blind people aren't supposed to know what they want. Isn't that weird?"

"Yeah . . . it really is . . . I never thought about it."

"Sometimes people ask me the dumbest things," Eileen said. She was smiling again.

"Like what?" Jeff asked, really interested.

"Like . . . how do you find your mouth with your fork? A lady actually asked me that once! Or, do you sleep with your eyes open or closed? That's another."

"No!" Jeff said incredulously. He was getting rather uncomfortable. He really didn't know what to say, and was sure that if he did open his mouth he'd be as guilty as those fools she was talking about. The next time, she'd probably have some more horrible stories to tell on him.

"Yes," Eileen was saying with equanimity. "Would you believe it? I was born this way, incidentally, in case you're wondering."

"Oh."

"Yeah . . . blind since birth," she said

flatly. She was simply stating a fact, and abruptly he realized that she was trying to put him at ease. He wished more fervently than he had ever wished before for the words he needed to let her know she was terrific.

The waiter came with their order and set it all down before them.

"Thanks," Jeff said. The man grunted and moved away again.

He watched her feeling carefully for her plate. Her light little fingers touched on the fat bun, the hot french fries, the pickled rings, and felt carefully for the container with the straw poking out.

"Can I help?" he asked her. But he was afraid that it was the wrong thing to say.

"No, thanks," she said pleasantly. "I don't need any help."

"I'm sorry."

"Hey, you don't have to be. Look, I just want to be treated like everybody else, okay?"

"Sure"

"You see that girl over there? A couple of booths back? You met her at the pool, remember?"

"Uh huh," he said, peering over at the table where Marge sat with Erik and the others.

"That's my friend, Marge. Now, would you ask her if she wanted help with her food?"

"No," he admitted, grinning back at her. "Hey, how did you know she was here?"

"I heard her when we passed by on our way

in. Anyway, I'll show you how I manage my food, if you're interested?"

"Oh, yeah, I am."

Well, this table is a clock."

"A clock?"

"Yes. See . . . my plate is at six o'clock, and you're opposite me at midnight. And my plate is a clock, too. My cheeseburger's here at twelve o'clock . . . my shake's at two o'clock . . . here . . . and my fries" — her fingers were deft and touched each item as she named it — "and my fries are at nine o'clock."

"Neat!" Jeff said.

"Where's the salt?" she asked him.

He twisted his head around to see it from her point of view. "Uh . . . at eleven o'clock," he said.

She reached out and found it, and sprinkled a bit on her potatoes.

"Thanks," she said. And then she laughed that nice low chuckle of hers, and said, "Nothing to it, see?"

He laughed, too, and somehow they were talking, a little bit.

She asked all the questions, of course, but he was able to contribute a few words of his own now and then. She had made him feel a lot more relaxed than he usually did, and he wasn't worried any more that he might say something really stupid. She'd heard all the stupid remarks before, and knew how to cope

49

with them. Anyway, he really forgot about her problem when they got into talking about the difference between courses at Eastern High and Western High. She even got him talking about how and why he wanted to be an engineer.

He walked her home. He was pleased to notice that she didn't bother taking out her white stick again, but put her hand through his arm as though they were old friends. She knew the way, and really led him down the four winding streets to her house.

Even the silences weren't uncomfortable with her. It was nice, just walking and feeling the late afternoon sun on their faces.

"What color are your eyes?" she asked him.

"Blue," he answered.

"Me, too," she said. Color's the hardest thing."

"What do you mean?" he asked her.

"I mean the hardest thing to visualize. What's blue, for example?"

"Well . . . the sky. . . ."

"No, no. I mean . . . what *is* blue? What's it look like?"

He was really silent now. Was there anyone on earth who could answer that question? He wondered.

She chuckled. "Stumped, huh?" she asked him.

"I guess so!"

"It's the thing I miss most, I guess . . . color. . . ." She said it without self-pity or bitterness or expecting any reaction from him; she just stated it, a fact. A fact that he had never in his life even thought about.

"Hey," he said after a moment, "you never told me what you want to do after you graduate. We talked about me being an engineer, but I didn't even ask you what you want to be."

"Oh . . . a lawyer, I think . . . or maybe a model. The kind that just stands around looking glamorous, and they take pictures of you." He didn't know whether she was kidding or serious. She was pretty enough to be a model, and he wondered how to tell her that, or whether he should, even. Probably everybody told her that, and she'd think it was just a line or something.

She slowed down and stopped in front of a medium-sized brick house with a long flight of steps leading up to it.

"This is where I live," she said. "Uh . . . want to come in?"

"Oh . . . oh, no thanks," he answered, suddenly shy again. "I guess I'd better get home."

"Okay," she said. "I had fun. Thanks for the cheeseburger and everything."

"I enjoyed it, Eileen . . . a lot."

"My friends call me Lee," she said.

"Lee."

"Well . . . so long, Jeff. See you." She turned to go up the stairs, holding lightly to the railing at one side.

"Hey . . . Eileen? I mean, Lee?"

She turned around and waited. "Yeah?"

"Uh . . . listen . . . do you want to go to the park on Sunday? You know, just walk and look at the animals?" He could have bitten off his tongue — look at the animals, terrific thing to say to a blind person. But she answered with real pleasure and sweetness.

"I'd love it," she said.

"I'll call you."

"Okay. Bye, Jeff."

"Bye. . . . Bye, Lee."

He waited until she had gone inside, and then he turned to walk slowly back to the bus stop near her school. He had a lot to think about.

That night at dinner, he explained to his mother and dad how blind people manage their food.

"So you did find things to talk about," he father said, "I told you. It's not so hard, is it?"

"I think it depends on the person you're talking to, doesn't it, Jeff?" his mother said. He nodded yes.

"I'm sure she's a very nice girl," his mother said.

"Are you going to ask her to the dance, son?" his father wanted to know.

"I don't know. I mean . . . I don't even know her. I only saw her once . . . twice. At the pool and this afternoon. I don't know whether I'd want to spend a whole evening with her. It's a little bit awkward, you know. When someone's blind, I mean. Lots of things you have to think about that you never thought of before."

"Like what?" his father wanted to know.

"Like . . . well, like colors. She never saw colors. Can you imagine what it would be like not to know what colors are? She asked me what blue was. How do you answer that?"

There was silence at the dinner table, and then Jeff's mother got up and started clearing away the dishes. "Maybe you shouldn't see too much of her," she commented quietly. "There must be lots of nice girls at your own school, Jeff. Isn't there anyone it would be . . . well . . . easier to be with?"

"He's not going to marry her," his father said sharply.

"I don't mean that there's anything wrong with taking out a person who's blind . . . of course not! It's just . . . well . . . Jeff doesn't need someone else's problems right now. He's got enough of his own, it seems to me."

"What problems?" his father asked her. "What problems has Jeff got?"

"I don't have any problems," Jeff said. "I

53

just found a girl I can kind of talk to a little bit, so what's the big deal?"

"She's blind," his mother said, not unkindly but looking worried.

"So you think everybody ought to stay out of her way, like it was contagious or something?" Jeff shot out angrily.

"Jeff!"

"I saw her supposed best friend ditch her this afternoon to be with some guy instead. They were talking over her head like she wasn't even there. I think that's rotten," Jeff said heatedly.

"Of course it's rotten," his mother said. There was pain in her voice, and sympathy, too. "But that doesn't mean you have to make up for someone else's behavior. You don't have to take the girl out just because someone else ditched her."

"That's not why I took her out. Anyway, I didn't take her out, we just had a burger after school, like everybody else. And it wasn't out of sympathy. I like her, she's bright and funny and . . . well, she's pretty, too, and I can sort of talk to her."

"I think that's great, Jeff." His father's words were addressed to him, but the look he gave across the table was meant for Jeff's mother. She got the message and said no more about it. When she was in the kitchen, Jeff turned to his dad and asked something that had been on his mind for quite a while.

"Dad, do you think everyone else is going to think about it the way Mom does? If I did take Lee to the dance, wouldn't people think I couldn't get any other date, or something? That I was doing it out of sympathy?"

"Jeff . . ." His father started to say something, but then it all got dissolved in another one of his pep-talk cliches. "Trust yourself, Jeff. Do what you think best."

Jeff sighed and stood up. He finished clearing off the dishes: the roast beef at seven o'clock, the potatoes at three, and the carrots right in the middle of the dial.

CHAPTER 5

"Phone for you, Lee!" her sister sang out from the kitchen. She handed over the receiver with her hand over the mouthpiece and her face in a state of wonder and excitement.

"It's a boy!" she whispered as Eileen came in and held out her hand for the phone.

Eileen grinned at the expression in Lucy's voice. She put her own hand over the receiver to whisper back, "Is it the President?"

"Go on, talk to him," her sister hissed, and noisily left the room.

"Hello?"

"Uh . . . hello . . . uh, Lee?"

"Yes. Hi, Jeff."

"Uh . . . how are you?"

"Fine, terrific. Isn't it a beautiful day?"

"Uh . . . yeah . . . I guess so. I haven't been out yet."

"Oh, neither have I, but I can feel the sun

pouring through the house here. The radio says it's mild and chances of precipitation are zero."

"Uh . . . good."

There was a little silence. Then she said, "Do you still want to go to the park? Or have you changed your mind?"

"No! I mean, sure I still want to go. Do you?"

"Yes. I think it's safe. I mean, the radio also said that the air is safe to breathe today."

Jeff laughed. He had a nice laugh, she thought. Nice and easy, when he wasn't being too shy to let it out.

"Should I pick you up?" he asked.

"Oh, you don't have to. Why don't we meet somewhere, halfway? I mean, the park is between the east side and the west side, so I'll meet you halfway, okay?"

"Sure. Whcre?"

"Uh . . . how about the bear cage? That's the easiest for me to find, because of the smell, you know." She was laughing, too, and he knew it was just a joke. She probably knew her way around the park, the whole city, maybe, better than most people.

"Okay, the bear cage at noon?"

"Terrific. See you then," she said.

"Okay. Uh . . . bye."

"Bye, Jeff."

"Who was it? Who is he?" her sister said eagerly, popping her head around from the doorway into the dining room.

"Couldn't you tell from listening?" Eileen retorted cheerfully. "Just a boy. Nobody special."

"You got a date with him? Do you think maybe he'll take you to the dance?"

"Lucy, will you please stop making a federal case out of it? We're only going for a walk in the park. Big deal. Hey, can I borrow your turtleneck sweater, the blue one?"

"Sure! It'll look neat with your new corduroy skirt."

"Thanks. I'm just going to wear my old jeans, if it's all the same to you."

Lucy followed Eileen up the stairs to their room, and chattered while they were getting dressed and cleaning up their room.

"Where's my hairbrush?" Eileen interrupted her sister's steady stream of talk to ask.

"I know two boys who go to Western, but neither one of them is named Jeff. Some of the kids think the guys over there are snooty, you know, brainy and too serious for the morons we go to school with, but I . . . oh, gosh, I'm sorry, Lee. I didn't put it back where it belongs. Here. It was on the windowsill."

"The windowsill?"

"Yeah . . . I was using it when the paper boy came and I leaned out the window to holler at him not to throw it in the bushes, and I guess I left the brush there. I'm sorry."

"It's okay. I know it's not normal for a girl your age to keep everything as neat as you have to because of me. Forget it."

"Well, here it is. Want me to brush your hair for you?"

"Lucy, I am not going to Westminster Abbey to be crowned. I'm going to the park, where I go practically every Sunday of my life. I don't care if my hair is parted crooked, honest, I don't."

"Your hair looks great."

"Thanks."

"Want me to walk you over to the park? I mean, I don't have anything else to do."

"You just want to get a look at Jeff," Eileen laughed.

"Yeah," Lucy admitted.

"No."

"Okay! I just asked."

"Look, I promise to introduce you to him before I marry him, okay?"

"I'm sorry, Lee."

"I don't blame you for being curious about what he looks like. I am, kind of, myself."

"Well . . . I could describe him for you."

"Some other time, Luce."

"Okay. Hey, have fun."

"Thanks. I will."

Eileen walked to the park alone, loving the feel of the warm autumn sun on her face, taking her time. She arrived at the bear cage a little early, and sat down on the bench to wait. She flipped open the little cover of her watch and felt quickly for the numerals — only a few minutes to wait.

But he was early, too.

"Hi, Lee."

"Hi." She was holding her white stick loosely in her hand, and as he sat down next to her she folded it and slipped it into her shoulderbag.

"Let's walk," she said, smiling.

They stood up and she took his arm. He wondered if he should say something, but there really didn't seem to be any need for it. They passed someone who was playing a radio very loudly.

"Do you like to dance?" she asked him.

"Well, I'm not too great at it but I enjoy it. Yeah, I guess so," he said lamely.

"I *love* it," she said. "That's the hustle they're playing."

"Right!" Jeff said. They walked on past the blaring sound and came up in front of the lion's cage. The great male lion was pacing and suddenly emitted a low, menacing roar.

Eileen laughed. "That's a lion," she said.

"It sure is."

"When I hear that, I expect a movie to start," she said, and Jeff laughed, too.

They wandered along the walkway past all the animals in their cages and the open areas separated from the people by deep trenches. At the elephant pit, Eileen let go of Jeff's arm to buy some peanuts from the machine, and he waited until she came back the few steps to his side. Then she held out her hand and the biggest elephant came lumbering over to take the offering from her. His great moist hairy nostrils at the end of his trunk tickled her palm, and she laughed again.

"That's a vacuum cleaner! Right?"

"It sure is!" he said with a chuckle. "Hey, that's terrific, what an imagination!"

"Well, I guess I see things differently from most people, in my mind, I mean. Like . . . well, what would you compare an elephant to?"

"An elephant? Well, let's see! Let me think! Gee, I don't know. An elephant's an elephant. Maybe you could say his mouth's too big for that peanut. He wolfed it down like . . . like the ocean opening up for a minnow. How's that?"

"Great!" she laughed. "You've given me a marvelous image to think about."

"And you, too. A vacuum cleaner! You know, you're absolutely right. I just never heard it or felt it like that. I guess I was just looking at it and seeing the same thing every time, and never using my imagination at all. But you — " He cut himself off before he said something awful. But she leaped at it.

"But I don't get bogged down by seeing

things the way they are, so I can just let my thoughts run loose and free. That's not so bad, is it?"

She was happy, he could tell. Happy that he had said so much. Gosh, where did he find so much to say? He could hardly believe it was him doing all that talking.

They strolled some more, around the elephants' yard and up near the cage where the gorillas lived.

"Gee, they look sad." Jeff said.

"Who?"

"I'm sorry!" He'd done it now. For a minute, he had just plain forgotten.

"Don't be," she said easily. "Who looks sad?"

"The gorillas. I hate seeing them in cages."

She nodded. "I know what you mean. It is sad."

They kept on walking and came to the edge of the zoo area, where the walkway widened and split off into different directions. There were the steps leading down to the fountain and the tunnel that went under the transverse toward the ball fields, and the start of the bike path that went all around the park. Jeff saw the red umbrella that fluttered gaily over the stand where they rented bikes, and he had a sudden idea.

"Hey, how about a bike ride?" he asked her.

Eileen grinned. "I'd love it, but I'll have to ride on your handlebars," she answered.

"No . . . they've got a bicycle built for two. How about that? Think you could manage if I did the steering?"

"Oh, sure! What a great idea! I'd absolutely love it!"

He was pleased with himself for thinking of it. They checked out the tandem bike, and after a lot of laughter and a couple of false starts, they got the hang of it and were off down the first sloping hill.

"It's terrific! It's marvelous!" Eileen sang out from behind him as they pedaled. The wind was blowing their hair, and the first downhill slope gave way to a widely angled curve, then an uphill grade, and a long low sweep on level ground around the outermost baseball diamond.

As they came into the flat stretch, Eileen tried to pump the pedals faster, and Jeff could feel the weight of her body shift as she leaned forward, urging more and more speed. He laughed and clutched the handlebars tightly, steering down the center of the wide path and hoping no one was coming at high speed around the next curve toward them. They passed everyone going in their direction. The safest thing to do was stay dead center as they careened toward the turn. He slowed, instinctively.

"No!" she shouted from behind him, "don't brake!"

"Okay," he shouted back, and gritted his

63

teeth as they swung wide around the curve. Eileen was laughing and shouting.

"This is fun!"

The bike picked up speed on a long down-grade now. Her feet were pushing against his cautionary efforts to slow down. The two sets of pedals were correlated and since he had promised not to brake, he didn't want to spoil her fun. But it was getting a little bit hairy, spinning toward the turns and whizzing past everyone, not knowing what was coming in the opposite direction, or whether some little kid or a dog was going to decide to cross the path in front of them.

"Faster." Eileen was shouting. "More! More!"

His hands were sweaty against the hard rubber grip of the handlebars, and the green leaves of the trees as they flew by seemed to whirl around and over them in a frantic kaleidoscope of motion and color and darting bolts of sharp jagged sunlight. His instincts shouted slow down, but behind him Eileen was laughing and urging even more speed.

"Come on!" she shouted. "It's wonderful! Faster, Jeff!"

Suddenly he caught a glimpse of silver and blue flashing in their path. He swerved to avoid the oncoming bike, and automatically his hands and feet braked. They avoided a collision by a few feet, and came to a stop at the edge of the curb.

"Hey, what's the matter?" she asked. "What are you doing?"

"I'm stopping," he answered.

"No!" she said. Disappointment made her voice drop low again after the high excitement, and he felt bad about that. Really terrific times were probably few and far between in her life, and here he was spoiling her fun. But damn, it was dangerous. Couldn't she see that? Well, couldn't she sense it, anyway?

"Why'd you stop?" she asked. Jeff, standing astride the bar, half turned around to look at her. She was still perched on the high rear seat with her feet on the pedals, ready to start up again, impatient with him.

"It was dangerous," he said.

An expression close to disgust crossed her face. "Oh, so you were worried about me. I told you, Jeff, treat me like everybody else! Can't you understand?"

She was really angry, and that made him angry, too. If she wanted to be treated like everybody else, how come she was asking him to risk his neck, and hers, too? She wasn't just like everybody else; anybody could have seen that they were going too fast for that bike path. But she couldn't see that, of course not, so that made her a little different from everybody else, didn't it?

It was getting very complicated.

"Wait a minute," he said firmly. "I was worried about *me*, okay?" He saw her anger turn into something a little like chagrin, but she quickly covered it up with her usual smile. He softened at once. And you, too," he added.

"Party pooper," she said softly.

"No kidding, Eileen, I . . ."

"Call me Lee."

"Okay, *Lee*. I just . . ."

"I like to be called Lee, especially by my friends."

"You're changing the subject," he said, staring at her. She was completely sunny again, and he realized suddenly that it was her way of apologizing. She was a real mixture of lots of things, this girl, just like everybody else.

"Yup," she said, laughing now. "Nicknames are a much more interesting subject. What's yours?"

He thought for a minute and looked down at his hand still gripping the brake. He let it ease back, and his knuckles turned a normal color again. "I don't have a nickname," he said.

"Then I'll just have to make one up, won't I?" she laughed.

"Okay."

"How about . . . um . . . Chicken?" she teased.

He grinned, realized she couldn't see that he'd forgiven her, and let the grin develop into a sound. Then, suddenly, without warning, they both started to laugh, and it was like racing down that hill . . . impossible to stop. They laughed and laughed and finally started to gasp and catch their breath, and somehow they were wonderfully free — and hungry.

"How about a hot dog?" he asked her.

"Oh, yeah, wonderful."

"Okay, we'll ride round to the end of the path, where we got the bike. It's not far now. Slowly," he added.

"Very slowly," she nodded solemnly.

"Right."

He got back on and steered them onto the path, and they rode sedately all the way around the track to the entrance. Behind him, she was letting him set the pace now, and murmuring only occasional comments, like: "I'll bet six turtles and a snail passed us. So glad you're not a reckless driver, old chap. I could have sworn the wind was blowing before!"

He laughed comfortably at her jibes, and knew he didn't have to say anything at all. When they reached the bike stall, she murmured, "Goodness, home already? It's still daylight!" He handed her down off the bike and returned it, and then they ate two hot dogs each and two sodas and shared a large bag of potato chips.

"Want to walk some more?" he asked her.

She flipped open her watch and felt for the time. "Sure," she said, "if you do."

They sauntered along the mall, her hand through his arm, and suddenly she stopped and turned to him.

"Hey . . . do me a favor?" she asked.

"Sure," he said.

"I want to feel what you look like."

She held her two hands up in front of her, fingers extended tentatively toward him.

"Okay?" she asked, not moving until he answered.

"Sure."

Her hands moved up slowly and her light, delicate fingers traced his forehead, his nose, cheekbones, the edges of his mouth, and his chin.

He felt a little funny, standing there in the middle of the mall, with people walking in all directions around them, and having her touch him like that. But actually, nobody seemed to be paying any attention. He tried to be casual. Could she feel the heat rising in his face?

"Well?" he said when she had taken her fingers away.

"Well," she answered, "your nose is kind of big."

"Thanks a lot."

"And your ears stick out."

"No they don't!"

She laughed; and he felt like saying some-

68

thing about how pretty she was. But he didn't.

"A little, they do," she insisted, nodding her head.

He put his hands over his ears, feeling them, trying to figure out what they felt like in relation to the rest of his head, to a person who'd never see them. She must have known exactly what he was doing; she was standing there smiling and waiting for his answer.

"Well . . . a little, maybe. Not so's you'd notice, though," he admitted.

"Hey, that's a nice smile," she said, as if she could really see his expression just then.

"I'm glad you like *something*."

"All in all," she said as she turned from him to begin walking again, "it's a nice face." She put her hand through his arm again, lightly.

"Think so?" he asked. It wasn't just small talk; he really wanted to know.

"A really nice face," she said, nodding her head.

"Well, thanks," he said. He was grinning and silent for a minute as they walked. "You had me worried there for a while," he said.

She was silent then, and he started to wonder whether it was in fact his turn. Should he say something about her looks? About her nice hair, and her smooth soft-looking skin, or her chin that was kind of pointy in a nice way, or her clear, gentle blue eyes. Go on, say something wonderful to a blind girl about how nice her eyes are. Terrific.

"C'mon, Nice Face," she said after a while, smiling still, "we'd better start for home."

"Okay," he said, and that was all. She must know how pretty she was, plenty of people must tell her all the time. Pretty and special. But on the way to her house, all his old problems of trying to think of something to say came back to him, and he was kind of relieved when they said good-bye in front of the steps.

"I had a nice time, Jeff. Thank you," she said.

"So did I," he answered.

"Bye."

"Bye, Lee."

He hadn't even said he'd call her. Well, he wasn't all that sure he would.

He turned to walk to the bus stop, and then changed his mind. He headed back to the park instead, to cut over to his side of town. It was a long walk but he had an awful lot to think about.

CHAPTER 6

His father was washing the car in the driveway. Jeff came outside and started to help. He grabbed one of the rags and started moving it around on the suds that covered the hood, not really mopping up the excess, just going through the motions. His mind was on something else.

"Hi, Dad."

"Hi, son. How's life?"

"Okay . . . pretty good."

"Here, take the hose on that side."

Jeff reached across and turned the nozzle on the soapsuds.

"Hey, Dad?"

"Yeah?"

"You know that dance I was telling you about the other day?"

"What about it? That's enough water, try a dry rag. Here."

Jeff tried to concentrate on the gleaming finish of the car. But he kept wiping the same circle over and over. His dad realized that he wasn't going to get exactly professional-level help in the car-wash department today. He stopped soaping his side and looked over at Jeff.

"What about the dance, Jeff? Did you decide to ask someone?"

"Well, I haven't actually decided. . . ."

"What's the problem, son? Hey, the hose is getting your shoes wet, better hand it over to me."

"Oh . . . uh . . . sorry. No, it's okay, I'll do the tires." Jeff bent down and focused his attention on the wheel. His dad couldn't see his face.

"Okay, Jeff, let's talk, how about it?" The water from the hose trickled to a stop as his dad turned off the faucet at the side of the garage. He walked back to Jeff's side of the car, and stood there, waiting for Jeff to talk to him.

"Well, it's a pretty important dance. It's a a joint one between the two schools, Eastern and Western."

"Yes. After the game, right? When is it, in about two weeks?"

"Yeah."

"What's the problem, Jeff?"

Jeff looked up at his dad's kind eyes. He

stood up and said what was on his mind. "I've been thinking of taking someone."

"Who? That nice girl you've been seeing?"

"Eileen. She *is* nice. But . . ." The moment of feeling like he could say anything to his dad had passed; he was stammering again.

"But what, Jeff?"

"But, like I told you, she's blind."

"Yes, I remember your mentioning it."

"So . . ." It seemed to Jeff that the problem was obvious; what more could he say about it?

His dad just looked at him, waiting. "So?" he said finally.

Jeff looked away from the concerned, but uncomprehending eyes of his father. It was probably just not possible for a fully grown man to get into the hassles of someone halfway between kid and . . . whatever.

"You'll have to spell it out for me," his dad said gently. "I'm sorry, but I don't understand the problem. Come on, spit it out."

"Well . . . I feel funny about asking a blind girl to a dance," Jeff blurted out. "Everyone would be staring at us. They'd think I was desperate for a date, taking a blind girl and all, like I couldn't do any better."

His father looked sad, as if he was disappointed with him. He was. His voice was quiet and serious. "You're ashamed to be seen with her," he said flatly.

Jeff could only nod his head. He was ashamed to even admit it, but there it was. It was true.

His father sighed. "Well," he said, "at least it's an honest feeling. Not one I particularly admire, but honest."

Jeff flinched, and then looked his dad in the eye. "I still feel bad about it," he said, almost in a whisper.

"Do you enjoy her company? Do you have fun together?"

"Yes."

"She has other friends, doesn't she?"

"Oh, sure. I mean, I guess so."

"Didn't you mention someone being kind of cruel to her once . . . something like that?"

"Oh, yeah. Her girlfriend went off and left her to go with some guy. I mean, they were making signals over her head. You know, like she couldn't see them, only she knew. But what's that got to do with it? I mean, I wouldn't hurt her feelings like that: I . . . I just . . . well, maybe she would feel funny, too, I don't know."

"Feel funny about being with you, you mean?

Well . . . no, I guess that's not it."

"You mean she might catch your vibrations, sense that you were the one who felt funny. Isn't that what you mean?"

Jeff was miserable. Why had he ever

brought it up? It was awful, talking about stuff like this. And yet he had to figure it out somehow. His feelings were in a terrible jumble. His dad was no help at all, only making it worse, more complicated.

"Jeff."

"Yeah?"

"I guess you don't have a very good opinion of yourself."

Startled, Jeff stared at his father. "Huh?"

"I mean, what you're basically saying is that what other people might think is more important than what you think."

"What?"

"You like the girl, you have fun with her, you enjoy her company and . . . is she pretty?"

"Oh, yeah . . . very. She really is. She laughs a lot, and her face kind of lights up. She's really pretty. And she said I have a nice face. Whatever that means."

"Now how would she know that?" his dad asked.

"She ran her fingers over my face. Said my ears stick out, but I don't think she really meant it. Made me laugh."

"Were you self-conscious when she did that? Were you in public, with other people around?"

"Uh, yeah . . . in the park. Yeah, I was kind of self-conscious, I guess. I mean, standing there in the middle of the mall and having this person touching your face. Well, it wasn't so bad."

"Why? Because you were thinking more of her than of yourself?"

"I . . . yeah, I guess maybe."

His dad spoke very thoughtfully, very quietly, and seriously. "Jeff, how do you think she feels, all the time? She sounds like a nice girl, with the usual kind of sensitivity that a teenaged person has to live through. It must be kind of rough for her, don't you think?"

"Oh, yes! I know it is. But you see, she's had her whole life to adjust to it, and she's terrific, always smiling and making the best of things. She keeps saying she wants to be treated just like everyone else."

"Then why don't you try that?"

Jeff and his father shared a long look of . . . could it possibly be . . . understanding? Something like that. Jeff thought about what his dad was saying, and he started to get the message.

"And I wouldn't worry too much about what other people might or might not be thinking, Jeff, that only means that you don't think so highly of yourself."

"I guess so."

"I think your instincts are good, and you know what's right and what's wrong. How about a little more confidence in yourself?"

"Yeah. . . ."

"Think about it, Jeff."

"Yeah . . . hey, Dad?"

"Yes?"

"Thanks."

His dad grinned and stooped down to turn on the faucet again. He tossed the end of the hose to Jeff. "Here, let's get some of this soap off. It's starting to dry, bad for the paint job."

Jeff really concentrated on the car then. His dad was trying as hard as he could to be helpful, he knew that for sure. The least he could do to return the favor was work hard on the old Mustang. It didn't seem like much in return for what he suspected was very good advice. He wasn't sure whether he could take it, act on it, or not . . . but there was something to be said for some honest gut talk, and he was grateful for that. He thought about it all while he worked on the car, and he swabbed and rubbed and polished till he could see his own face clear as a mirror in the shining surface.

When they were finished, he went upstairs and dialed Eileen's number. She answered the phone herself this time.

"Hi, Lee."

"Oh, Jeff, hi. How was your math test?"

He'd noticed that about her. She always started off their conversations with a question, as if she knew it was hard for him to start off talking about nothing. He appreciated it a lot.

"Not bad," he answered. "I think I did okay. How're you doing?"

"Great. Terrific. Hey, Jeff?"

"Yeah."

"I've decided to tell you something about the other day. When we were bike-riding?"

"Oh, yeah, sure. What about it?"

"I'm sorry," she said in a very small voice. He could hardly hear her. He pressed the phone closer to his ear and waited, but all he could hear was her breathing.

"Hey, you don't have to say that."

"Oh yes I do. It's a very big deal for me, you know that?"

"What do you mean?"

"I made up my mind when I was very, very little, and I've stuck to it. This is the very first time in my life I've ever . . . . Well, I promised myself I'd never apologize for being blind. That's all." Her voice immediately resumed its cheerfulness, as if she was relieved to get it over with and wanted to go on to something else.

"Lee, I don't want you to apologize to me, not for that!" He was genuinely shocked, and something hurt deep down inside him, like a sharp, stabbing pain all of a sudden.

"Well, I acted stupid," she said.

"Yeah," he agreed. There was a silence at the other end; he couldn't even hear her breathing this time. Maybe she was holding her breath in shock, but then he heard her low soft laugh and he knew it was okay.

"Uh . . . you going to the pool tomorrow morning?"

"Sure," she answered promptly.

"Good. Well, then . . . I'll see you there."

"Not if I see you first, ha ha," she laughed, and he broke up.

"Boy, you're a character, you know that?" he said.

"I know."

"It's okay, though. I'm a little weird myself."

"Jeff?" she said after a little pause.

"Yeah?"

"I don't think you're weird. I think you're nice," she said and she hung up on him before he had a chance to think of an answer. He checked the mirror on the wall over the phone table. He wasn't blushing or anything, just grinning from ear to ear. Did they really stick out? He was whistling as he settled down to do his homework.

"Was that him?" Her sister wanted to know.

"Whom?" Lee teased.

"The Archbishop of Canterbury," Lucy said.

"No, alas! Just the Prince of Wales. Wanted to know if I was coming to the royal orgy tomorrow."

"You going to meet him at the pool?"

"Yeah, I guess so."

"Hey, terrific!"

"No, Lucy, don't ask me what I'm going to wear, okay?" They laughed and went arm in arm upstairs to their room. They were quiet for a while as they read at their separate desks. Eileen found it hard to concentrate on the Braille tapes in front of her. Her fingers were dutifully skimming the lines, but her mind was hopping around from one vague dreamy thing to another.

"Hey, Lucy?" she murmured.

"Yeah?"

"You know what I'd want to see more than anything, if I could just see one thing?"

"What?"

"My face."

Lucy put her ballpoint down and looked over at her sister. "You have a nice face," she said.

Eileen scowled, deliberately pulling one side of her mouth down and making lines in her forehead. "I don't think so," she said lightly.

"Oh, Lee, why not?"

Eileen heard the sympathy and concern in her sister's voice, and for once she let her feelings rush out. Her defenses couldn't always be up; she had to be honest sometimes, and here sister was . . . well, her sister.

"I don't have dates," she said slowly. "I

mean, I have friends and all . . . the kids seem to like me all right. . . . I'm busy, I have fun, but boys don't ever ask me out."

"What about Jeff?" Lucy asked.

"Yeah . . . what about Jeff? Eileen echoed. "He's just another friend."

"Oh, Lee!" Lucy was unexpectedly close to tears, but she tried not to let her sister know it. She was supposed to be the strong one; the older and wiser sister for Eileen to lean on. "Hey," she said, "give it time. Maybe it'll develop into something. You never know."

"But . . ."

"You like him, don't you?"

"Well, sure, he's very nice. He's very shy, but I think I've made him feel more at ease than he was at first. Yeah . . . he's okay."

"And he likes you, too, I can tell. If a boy keeps calling and wanting to be with you, that's the sign."

"But he won't ask me to the dance."

"Now how do you know that? If he's shy, maybe he's just trying to get his courage together."

"Courage? To ask a girl to a dance?"

"Well . . . some boys take longer than others.

"Lucy . . ."

"Yeah?"

"If I were really ugly, really disgustingly homely, would you tell me?"

"Wouldn't I just! You could hear me retch

every time you came near me. What a dumb question."

"No, I mean really. Suppose I was just . . . moderately homely?"

"I'd tell you. I'd be the first. Haven't you ever heard of sibling rivalry?"

"Oh, come on, Lucy, I'm serious."

"I know, I'm sorry. Listen, Lee . . . you're really very attractive. Honest. Cross my heart."

"Like a movie star?" Eileen smiled wistfully, in the hopeless desert of her mind where she tried to imagine how people really looked. She'd never seen *anyone's* face.

"No, not like a movie star. Like, well, like a very pleasant, attractive person that anyone would like to be around. Honest."

"Not anyone. People sometimes feel really strange being around me. I know that much. But if I were really pretty, that wouldn't matter. I mean, my being blind wouldn't matter, would it? To a boy, I mean. Or . . . yes, I guess it would. It matters."

"You think that's why Jeff hasn't asked you to the dance? Pooh, I doubt that. He's just shy, like you said. Give him time, Lee."

"And what if he doesn't?"

"So . . ." But Lucy was at a loss to know what to say. She didn't want her sister hurt, but of course there was a big possibility that she'd never have dates. Lucy had seen the way people looked at Eileen when they first knew she was blind. Like she was some kind of two-headed monster with no feelings at all. Lucy had been hurt herself plenty of times, seeing how people treated her little sister. And Lee was so brave, so cheerful and . . . well, it just wasn't fair. It wasn't fair. She found herself wishing she could cast some kind of spell on that jerky Jeff and make him call, right this minute, and invite Eileen to the dance.

But she knew better than to try to call him and interfere at all. Eileen was too sharp for that. No one could help her, and no one had better try, not that way.

"You know what Mom always says," was all Lucy could come up with. "What's important is the person inside you."

"Yeah. She's right."

"Of course. Mom's always right."

"Right!"

"Right!"

The two sisters laughed, and Lucy jumped up from her chair and went to put her hands lightly on her sister's shoulders. "Listen, it's true, you know. You're terrific inside."

"Yeah, way down deep I'm beautiful."

"It's true, Lee. And any boy you're going to like . . . well, he'd have to be the kind of guy who'd feel that way, too."

"That's deep, Luce."

"Oh, yeah, way down deep I'm very deep."

"Hey, thanks, Lucy."

Lucy went back to her own desk and sat down again. She kept gazing across at Lee, though, wishing she could think of something more helpful to say.

"But on the surface . . ." Eileen mused out loud.

"On the surface, what?"

"What if I'm really homely?"

"What if the whole world is a glob of spit In the mouth of a dragon?"

Eileen laughed. "You do have a way of comforting a person," she said.

"Any time."

"Thanks, Luce."

They went back to their books, and the room was quiet for a long time, except for an occasional page being turned or the tiny puncture sounds of the Braille stylus punching out words as Eileen took notes.

Later, just before Lucy turned out the lights at bedtime, she brought up their conversation again, just for a brief word.

"Lee?"

"Mmmm?"

"You're not homely."

Eileen chuckled as she snuggled down against her pillow. "Neither are you," she said. "In fact, sometimes you're positively beautiful."

CHAPTER 7

Things were back to normal in the morning. Eileen reached for her hairbrush on the left-hand corner of the dresser and her hand came in contact with a crumpled candy-bar wrapper instead.

"Lucy, where's my brush now?"

Lucy muttered in her sleep and rolled over. Eileen went over to her sister's bed and reached down to shake her shoulder.

"Come on, Lucy, what'd you do with my brush? I'm going to be late."

"Late for what?" Lucy yawned.

"I'm going to the pool. I can't find my brush, for a change."

Lucy blinked up at her and closed her eyes again. "You don't have to brush your hair to go swimming," she murmured, and tried to go back to sleep.

Eileen shook her harder. "Look, Luce, I know it's a drag for you to have to keep everything exactly in a certain place, but you ought to be used to it by now. Come on, help me find my brush."

"It's there someplace," Lucy groaned and rose up like a massive mountain slowly erupting from a sea of bedclothes. She stood up and started to rummage around the room. "I don't mind your using it, but I really wish — "

"I know, I know. I'm sorry, Lee. Hold your horses, it's here someplace. I'll find it. What're you getting up this early for anyway on a Saturday morning?"

"It's the best time for the pool. Not so crowded."

"Yeah, and Jeff's going to be there," Lucy muttered. She yawned again, letting her annoyance come through.

"What's that supposed to mean?" Eileen asked.

"Nothing. Here's your brush. Now can I go back to sleep?"

"Thanks."

Their mother called from her room to ask what they were quarreling about this time.

"Nothing, Mom," Eileen called out. "We're not fighting."

"Can I go back to sleep now?" Lucy asked with exaggerated patience.

"Well, don't expect me to apologize because you keep losing my brush," Eileen whispered angrily.

"It wasn't lost. G'bye." Lucy snuggled down into the covers and Eileen made a fast pass at her hair with the brush. She set it down in its proper place and rushed out of the room and downstairs. She forgot her little bag with the swimsuit and had to go back for it, but finally she was on her way. It was another glorious day, and as she waited for the bus, she was thinking that soon the weather would turn crisp and cold. It was almost the end of football season already. Just two weeks to the big game between Eastern and Western . . . and the dance, of course.

She tried to put it out of her mind. The bus came and she climbed aboard. The driver greeted her cheerfully. She recognized his voice.

"Good morning, Mr. Lucas."

"Going swimming?"

"Sure. I go almost every Saturday."

"That's terrific, a kid like you. . . . I mean . . . here, there's a seat right there," the driver said kindly.

"No problem, Mr. Lucas, thanks," she said, and moved farther back to an empty seat near the rear door. The front seats were reserved for handicapped persons. Someone else might need it.

Marge and Pam and some of the other girls from her class were already there. They called to her as she emerged from the dressing room, and she joined their little group on the bench near the diving boards.

"Hey, it's crowded this morning, isn't it?" she said.

"Hey, Marge!" Erik's voice called out from the water. "Hurry up!"

"Okay!" Marge hollered back. "In a minute!"

"How's the water today?" Eileen asked.

"Crowded," Pam answered. "Full of nasty little boys."

"Hey, Marge!" Erik sang out from the shouts and laughter of the kids in the pool.

"Boys!" Marge said with a trace of irritation in her voice, but she started to get up to join him.

"Hey, you know that boy I've been seeing?" Eileen said casually.

"Jeff?" Marge asked. She stopped and waited.

"Uh-huh," Eileen said. "He says he likes to dance."

"He looked kind of clumsy to me," Pam said.

Eileen thought this over. "Well, I don't know," she said. "He's a pretty good swimmer. I was thinking . . . I was thinking of inviting him to the dance."

"Well, I think that'd be neat, Lee," Marge said enthusiastically.

"Gee, he seems a little goofy to me," Pam commented, and then quickly added, "but then, I don't know him."

Eileen was pretty sure Marge had given Pam a look that said volumes, as the novels always described certain kinds of looks.

"I don't know him very well, either," she said quietly. "Not really. Oh, well, it was just a thought."

"It sounds like a good idea to me, Lee," Marge said warmly. She was standing in front of them, and Erik was still calling to her petulantly from the water, but she was ignoring him for the moment.

"Yeah, sure," Pam said uncertainly, trying to sound more enthusiastic than she was. "Well," she said after a little silence, "I'm going swimming. You guys coming in?"

"In a minute," Eileen said cheerfully.

"Yeah, I'd better go in, or that creep Erik will drown himself. He's probably taking on water every time he opens his mouth to holler at me. What a nut!"

"I thought you liked him," Eileen laughed.

"I do!" Marge shouted over her shoulder as she moved toward the pool's edge. Eileen heard them both diving in, and there was a great deal of animated splashing and laughing from the deep end now. She'd wait until it was a little less crowded and boisterous before going in.

"Hi, Eileen. I mean, Lee."

"Hi, Jeff." She smiled up at him. He sat down on the bench next to her. She could tell that he had been in the water; his skin smelled damp and fresh from the chlorine, and he was breathing deeply as if he'd been doing fast laps or diving.

"It's crowded today, isn't it?" she said.

"Yeah."

The horseplay in the water grew wilder and there were shrieks of laughter, shouts and splashing noises at a high pitch. The kids were scrambling out of the pool and diving back in with great bellylaughs from the boys and outraged squeals from the girls, indicating that the boys were taking advantage of their strength in a time-honored game. They were throwing the girls in the pool, and there was a really deafening din of roaring and splashing and laughing and confusion.

"Oops, there goes Marge!" Eileen laughed. A familiar shriek was cut off with a resounding plop as another body hit the water.

"They seem to like getting thrown in," Jeff commented.

"Yeah," Eileen laughed. "They scream and try to run away, don't they, but not too much. . . . And then they laugh and climb back out for more."

"There's Mrs. Hays, your friend," he said. "She just came in."

"Looking this way?" Eileen asked.

"Uh . . . yeah, now she is."

Eileen waved her hand in the air briefly. A high-pitched squeal quite close by made Eileen laugh again. "That's my friend Pam," she said. "I guess Mark showed up."

Pam's giggles resounded over the general chaotic sounds as she swam back toward them after her unexpected dive.

"Sounds like fun," Eileen said.

Did she seem wistful? He stared at her, but her smile was the same as ever and she didn't seem to mind being on the sidelines. She never seemed to mind, but he knew her well enough now to know something else about her. She did mind. She minded a lot. He stood up and touched her hand, pulling her gently to her feet.

Suddenly he grabbed her two arms and shouted, "You're next!"

Without warning, he pushed her backwards into the water. Her scream was not like the other girls' screams. It was pure terror. She hit the water and went under. After a couple of seconds her head emerged, but she was open-mouthed in her panic, not knowing where she was, having no sense of orientation that made the world possible for her. She screamed again, but her mouth filled with water. She coughed and sputtered and flailed her arms wildly, sobbing in her terrifying aloneness.

Several of the kids bobbing around in the water tried to reach out to her, but she was too panicked to take a hand. She pushed them away and kicked and struggled, and her slim body sank again beneath the surface.

The lifeguard dove from his stand and came up next to her but she struggled with him furiously as he brought her to the surface. She pushed him away, too, and kept coughing and sputtering with the water in her throat and nose and mouth, angry in her dark unseeing fear.

Mrs. Hays was at the side of the pool next to Jeff. Her clear, sharp voice rose above the chaotic din.

"Over here, Eileen. Lee, this way. Over here. Lee!"

Somehow, Eileen kicked and flailed her way toward the edge, and her hand was grasped firmly by Mrs. Hays, who helped her to climb up onto the tiles.

"I'm okay, I'm okay," she gasped, shuddering. Mrs. Hays had her arm around Lee, but the frightened girl shrugged her away, "I'm all right," she insisted, trying not to sob. She pulled away and walked along the edge, her head held high, obviously wishing everyone would stop staring at her. She slipped on a wet tile and almost fell. Everyone in the circle around her leaned forward as one person to help her, but no one touched her. Eileen's pride forbade it. She caught herself and kept on walking, past the diving board and toward the bench along the wall.

Mrs. Hays came up behind her, holding a towel open.

"Here, Lee, take this towel. Come on. Dry yourself off," she said quietly.

Eileen shook her head, and pushed away from her friend and teacher. "I'm okay, please, please . . ." she said, embarrassed by the eyes she could feel on herself and by her own tears that wouldn't stop.

Jeff was standing there feeling like Frankenstein's monster, only he had no one to blame except himself. What was wrong with him; he was really grotesque. What a dumb thing to do, worse than dumb — criminal. A criminal act, that's what it was. Cruel, ugly, stupid and . . . stupid, stupid, stupid.

"Lee," he said painfully, "I'm sorry. I'm awfully sorry."

He was, unbelievably, close to tears himself.

She shook her head, not looking in his direction, but trying to hide her feelings, to catch her sobs and turn them into light bantering talk somehow. "It's okay," she said. "Honest, I'm fine."

He saw that she was terribly red in the face, and it wasn't only the terror and exertion of being nearly drowned. She was blushing, embarrassed.

"You said . . ." He couldn't seem to stop himself from talking now. He needed desperately to explain and to have her understand. "You said it seemed like fun," he said urgently. "You said you wanted to be treated like everybody else. I didn't want it to happen that way. Honest . . . I wouldn't . . ."

"Please," she said softly, almost pleading with him. "I just want to get out of here. I've got to get out of here."

She walked away from him quickly, but with her own special brand of dignity, alone. People had finally stopped their hushed and curious staring, and were starting to horse around in the water again. They weren't as loud and crazy as before, but at least they had stopped looking like they'd just witnessed a murder. Jeff stood there miserably, watching Eileen's straight firm back as she went toward the dressing room.

Mrs. Hays was at his side. She put her hand lightly on his arm. "Jeff?"

"Mrs. Hays . . . I'm sorry. She said . . . she wanted to be treated like everybody else, and . . ."

"Jeff, I think maybe it's time you and I had a little talk, okay?"

"Uh . . . sure."

"How about meeting me in the coffee shop across the street? In about . . . ten minutes?"

"Okay."

He was glad to get out of there. He didn't look at anyone while he was showering and dressing. He wondered if this was what convicts felt like before they got the lecture from the judge and sentencing.

He took a table near the door and waited for Mrs. Hays. She was smiling when she came in, not a happy smile especially but a warm one, as if to make him feel better. She sat down and they ordered two hot chocolates.

"I really feel bad." he said.

"I know you do," Mrs. Hays said gently.

"She's really angry with me, and she has a right to be. What a dumb thing to do."

"No, I don't think she's angry, Jeff. Not at you, anyway. She felt terribly embarrassed . . . in addition to being frightened. She hates to call attention to herself."

"Yeah, I know. I just didn't think."

"In a way, it was a compliment to her. And I'll bet she sees it that way, too, or she will when she gets over her fright."

"A compliment?"

"Yes. She'll understand that you really were treating her like everybody else . . . that maybe you forgot, for a minute, that she's blind. The way Lee feels about herself, that's quite a compliment."

"But . . . she's not like everybody else."

"That's what I wanted to talk about, Jeff. She wants to be, and she's wonderful about trying, but there are differences. Lee is still trying to come to terms with that."

"Mrs. Hays, how's someone like me supposed to know, if Lee herself doesn't even know? I mean . . . like what's okay and what's not okay? I don't want to feel like I'm walking on eggs all the time when I'm with her."

"Do you feel that way when you're with her?"

"No," he admitted. "But look what just happened. How was I supposed to know?"

Helplessly, he hunched over his steaming cup of chocolate and stared down into the untouched liquid. Mrs. Hays sipped at hers, but her eyes never left his troubled face.

"You really like Lee, don't you?" she asked.

"Well . . . yeah, but. . . . "

"But it's difficult."

"Yeah."

"Would it be easier with some other girl?"

He shook his head dolefully. "I never even could talk to any other girl. She's at least easy to talk to, most of the time."

"So . . . everybody has some kind of problem. It's not easy to be with anybody, really.

I mean, there are always certain adjustments to be made."

He looked up at her and nodded thoughtfully. He lifted the cocoa to his lips and tasted it. It was sweet and warming; made him feel better.

He set the cup down and talked. Really talked. He said exactly what was on his mind.

"It's hard to understand what it means to be blind," he said. "I mean to really understand it . . . isn't it? It's like being in a completely different world. I never thought about it before, but now I think about it a lot. Things look different to me, and every once in a while I think I understand . . . and then something happens like this stunt I just pulled. I mean, I can't really imagine what it's like for her. You work with blind people, don't you? How did you learn? Did you go to a special school, and what kinds of things do they teach you? Is it ever possible really to understand what it's like?"

Mrs. Hays nodded seriously. "Shut your eyes, Jeff."

"Huh?"

"That's right. Shut your eyes. Right. Now try keeping them closed for a while. Do you think you could find your way out of this restaurant, pay the check, find your way home, without opening them again, even once?"

"Wow! No, I guess not. I mean, I'm not used to it. Hey," he said, opening his eyes wide and staring across the table at her. "Is that how you learned? About what it's like to be blind? Keeping your eyes shut and trying to get around and do everything?"

Mrs. Hays nodded. "That's part of the training, yes. Things really are different when you can't see. It's a strange and unexpected world in ways a sighted person just couldn't anticipate."

Jeff's eyes bulged as a wild idea began to take shape in his brain. "How'd you do it?" he asked. "How'd you manage to keep your eyes closed all the time? How long did it take, you know, to find out . . . what it's like?"

"In the school where I trained, we wore patches over our eyes for days or even weeks at a time. The soft tape called moleskin that you can buy in the drugstore. We used to cut patches that would fit over our eyes and then put sunglasses over them, and carry white sticks, and actually go everywhere on our own. It's very difficult, but it does give you a sense of what that world is like."

"Yeah. . . ."

"Of course, knowing you can take the blinders off at any time and see again makes all the difference. There's no way, Jeff, that a sighted person can ever really know what it's like."

"But with those patches on . . ."

"Hey, don't get any ideas. It's not a game, you know."

"Of course not! I was just thinking. . . . What *would* it be like?"

"Jeff, the important thing is that you understand how difficult it is, sometimes, for Eileen. This morning she had a real fright, but it wasn't your fault. She has to learn, too, that she can't ask to be treated like everyone else. It's awfully hard, for her and for anyone who takes the trouble to be her friend."

"I'd like to be her friend. I'd take the trouble," he said slowly. An idea was starting to whirl around in his brain, crazy, maybe. His first thought was: would she be mad? Hurt? And then: would he have the nerve to do it?

Mrs. Hays signaled to the waiter to bring the check. Jeff started to dig in his pocket, but she indicated that she wanted to pay, and he murmured his thanks. His mind was really starting to spin now with a plan.

Out on the sidewalk, Mrs. Hays held out her hand to shake his. "Good-bye, Jeff."

"Uh . . . I really appreciate your talking to me like this, Mrs. Hays. I felt lousy about what happened, and now you've got me thinking that maybe . . . maybe I could even help Eileen, if she'd let me."

Mrs. Hays smiled. "Or maybe, just maybe, she could help you, too, Jeff."

"Huh?"

"I've got to run, there's my bus. Good-bye, Jeff. See you."

"Yeah . . . see you."

He was deep in thought as he turned to walk home and didn't even see the light turning red at the intersection. He stepped off the curb and was startled into leaping backwards when a large truck blared out at him seconds before it barreled across where he had been walking.

And he had his eyes open, too.

CHAPTER 8

"Lee? Can I come over and see you?"

"Sure, Jeff."

"You're not mad at me?"

"No."

There was a silence.

"You're sure?" he asked her.

"Oh, come on over, Jeff. Everybody's reading the Sunday papers and I'm making a banana cake. It should be just about ready to take out of the oven when you get here. I can smell it already. Come on over, you can have the first slice. See if it's poisoned or anything."

"Okay. Be right over."

He was horribly nervous, but he had made up his mind. He cut the two oval patches with a scissors and held them up to his eyes to make sure they fit, wide enough to cover all possible light that might come in through the edges. But before he actually stuck them over his eyes, he double-checked his clothes and his teeth and socks to make sure he was presentable; then he put his wallet and comb in his pocket and picked up the thin white cane he had bought. He wrapped the strap around his wrist and stood facing the front door. He didn't want to step out there. But he had made up his mind and he would do it. If people laughed at him or stared, that was part of what he was bargaining for, wasn't it? Anyway, if he couldn't see them maybe it'd be a terrific new sense of freedom, not even knowing if anyone was staring or laughing or not.

Maybe.

He placed the patches over his eyes, smoothed them down firmly, and placed the wide-framed sunglasses over them. He groped around for the handle to his own front door. The stick banged against his knees and then rammed the door, probably scratched the wood. Great start.

He was out on the sidewalk. Facing the street? Well, sure, he hadn't turned at all, the house was still behind him, that made the street straight ahead. At least, he didn't think he had turned. He tapped ahead of him on the cement with the point of the white stick. He took a step to one side, moved the stick

around, and it sounded for him, tap tap tap tap
nothing. The nothing was when the stick hit
the dirt at the edge of the walkway. Good.
Now he knew where the edge was. Just follow it right down to the street and then turn
left.

When his own sidewalk widened into the
public pathway, he made a decision. Part of
this learning process was to find out what the
limits were, how far one could reasonably
expect to go on one's own. In other words,
he smiled to himself ruefully, take a taxi instead of trying to hassle with the bus. After
all, it was his first day of being blind.

But how to get a taxi? How could you know
when one was coming down the street, or
whether it was empty or had a fare? He stood
on the curb and waited, one hand tentatively
held up in the air, in case an empty cab with
an alert driver happened by.

To his surprise, one did. A car pulled up
near him and a man's voice said, "Taxi,
Mister?"

"Yes, thanks," he said gratefully. He waved
the stick in the air, too high, it hit the side of
the cab. He moved closer and felt with his
hands until he found the door and the handle.
Funny, he'd never thought before about car
doors. Was the handle in the middle or toward
the back? He found it toward the back, opened
the door and got inside. He gave Eileen's ad-
dress and sat back with a huge sigh of relief.

Unprepared for the turn at the corner, the lurch sent him almost over on his side. He reached for the strap and hung on, for the first time in his life. Hands were becoming very important. Also ears. He listened to the sounds of the traffic and concentrated on the route the driver was taking. He said the street names over in his mind and they moved across town and turned into the park. He recognized the sweeping curves of the transverse and dimly heard the music from the carousel far over to one side.

Two stop lights, a left turn, and the taxi stopped.

"Is this it?" he said, sitting forward and reaching for his wallet. In answer, the cab jerked forward and began to move again. It had been a red light. Now the cab slowed again and stopped. The driver turned around and spoke to him.

"This is it, number 47," he said kindly.

"Uh, thanks," Jeff said. He opened the door of the cab and stepped out. Then he leaned toward the driver's window and asked, "How much?"

He'd have to take the driver's word for it, of course. He wondered if anybody was really unscrupulous enough to take advantage of blind people who couldn't check the meter, or add up a bill in a restaurant, or. . . .

"Two and a quarter," the driver said.

Jeff felt in his wallet. He had put the singles in front, the two fives behind. He held out two singles and fished in his pocket for change. He had no idea whether the fare was right or not; he'd never taken this particular ride before. He gave the driver three quarters and the two bills.

"Here," he said, waving the money in the direction of the driver's voice.

"Thanks. Can I help you up to the house, buddy?"

"No, thanks, I can manage."

The cab pulled away, and Jeff waggled the cane along the walk ahead of him. Grass, a little narrow trench — funny, he'd never noticed that, maybe there were flower seeds growing there, better be careful not to poke the ground and uproot them — more sidewalk . . . but it seemed vast, as he crossed the public path to head toward Eileen's house. He wasn't even sure he was still turned toward the house. His cane made an awful racket. He wondered if there was anyone around, watching him. What a fool he must look like, stumbling around this way in front of a blind girl's house. Would someone think he was making fun of her? Her parents, or her sisters, or neighbors might be watching him and wondering who he was. Could he pass for a blind person or was it obvious that he was pretending. But he really couldn't see, not anything.

He stumbled, almost fell. There was even a

special skill to using the stick. He tapped it back and forth ahead of him, finding the edges of the narrow sidewalk leading to her house. He centered himself to walk straight along it until the stick banged against the first step.

He'd never realized before how high a single step is. He lifted his foot and tentatively toed in, feeling for a secure footing. His hand groped for something to hold onto; there was a railing and he clung to it as if it were a lifeline, a rope tow for a skier going up a mountain. The flight of steps really did feel like a mountain; he had no idea how many steps, but he vaguely remembered that the house was set rather high on its foundation and the stairs were steep and high. He planted both feet on the first rise and let the stick point straight down before him, feeling for the height of the next one.

He fell a couple of times, saving himself by clinging to the railing and pulling himself back up. He thought he might never get to the top of the steps; the urge to rip the tape off his eyes came over him like the thought of food to a starving person. And he hadn't even been blind for a half-hour yet! He forced himself to keep on climbing the endless Mt. Everest of steps. His feet went in awkward directions as if he couldn't control them, and his whole body tended to bend close to the ground; he wanted to crawl up the steps on his hands and knees, feeling the security of the surfaces beneath him with both hands and his knees. But he stumbled and stayed on his path, managing to balance one way or another on a pair of feet which were suddenly alien to him.

He reached the top of the steps; the stick swung in the air before him with no more obstructions. He put out his hand to find the door.

There was one more step, a small rise of only a couple of inches, just before the door. The stick passed over it. Jeff's feet shuffled, and tripped. He went sprawling on his side. For a horrible second he envisioned himself rolling down the concrete steps, that sharp mountain-high precipice he had just scaled. But he had fallen forward, and his shoulder wrenched sharply against the door itself.

"Ow!" He had lost hold of the stick. His hands groped out for it, feeling everywhere. Cold concrete, a doormat, the firm barrier of the door itself. . . . Had the stick rolled down the steps?

He got to his feet slowly, sliding his hands up along the flat surface of the door, and composed his face as well as he could. He wondered if he looked scared. He knocked with his knuckles on the door, tentatively at first, then louder.

No one answered. He knocked again, and again.

"Hello? Hello!" he shouted. Now he was

actually pounding on the hard wood. She was expecting him, why didn't she answer?

At last he heard someone's footsteps inside, and felt a subtle gust of air as the door opened a crack.

"Who is it?" Eileen asked. She sounded annoyed.

"It's me . . . Jeff," he answered. It came out like a sigh, or a groan.

"Why didn't you ring the bell?" she asked. She opened the door wider; he felt the warmth from inside the house reaching out to welcome him.

" . . . I couldn't find it," he admitted.

He heard the puzzlement in her voice. "Why not?" she asked him.

Jeff blushed. "I . . . I'm blind," he said quietly.

"*What?*"

"Lee . . . I've put tape over my eyes. I can't see."

He waited. Would she be angry? Hurt? Disgusted? Would she send him away, tell him off?

He felt her hand on his, guiding him inside. "Well, you'd better come on in," she said. "Be careful, there's a little table just inside the door on your right."

She led him inside and they sat down in the living room. He'd never been in her house, and wondered what it was like. You could tell so much about people from their houses, whether they lived with lots of light or kept the shades and curtains drawn; whether they were neat or liked a bit of clutter; whether they had old, comfortable things around them or . . . but he couldn't tell any of those things. He was sitting on a sofa, and she was nearby, facing him, sort of to one side. There was a table in front of him, low and far enough away from the couch so there was room for his legs. She had guided him around it when they came in.

"Now, what's this about?" she asked. She sounded friendly, warm, interested. Not angry at all. But really curious.

"I feel so bad about yesterday. You know, what happened at the pool . . . and I thought maybe if I knew more what it was like for you. . . . I just wanted to understand more. I hope you don't think I'm crazy."

"No," she said softly.

"So I decided I wanted to know how it felt to be blind. I didn't want to have to guess."

"Gee . . ." Eileen said. She sighed, and he knew it was all right.

"I feel real bad for being so dumb with you all the time, making mistakes and all."

He was astounded, suddenly. She was chuckling.

"Why are you laughing?" he asked her. Maybe he was wrong, maybe he couldn't trust the vibrations he could have sworn were so friendly and warm. She was laughing at him.

"I'm laughing because you're shouting," she said.

"I am?" He realized it was true. He lowered his voice and repeated, "I am?"

"Yeah . . . that's one of the tricky things about being blind, Jeff. Learning just how loud to talk."

"Gee," he said, "I never knew that."

"Well, it's true."

"You don't mind? My doing this, I mean?"

"Mind? No. No, I don't mind. I . . . I'm . . . no, I don't mind."

"Will you help me?"

"Sure! Want to go for a walk?"

"I . . . okay. But I'd better warn you, I darn near broke my neck coming up your steps just now. I'm really clumsy."

"Come on," she said. "Let's go to the park. It's a beautiful day . . . well, maybe a little bit overcast, but I don't think it'll rain."

He got to his feet, following the sound of her voice as she moved toward the door. "How do you know that?" he asked her curiously.

"Heard it on the radio," she laughed.

She led him out of the door and carefully down the steps.

"Oh . . . I had a stick, but it got away from me. Should be somewhere around here," he said.

"We'll find it. Hold onto the railing on your

side, and when we get down I'll poke around for it. Can't have gotten far. There are twelve steps, a little one first and then two paces to the real steps. Got the railing?"

"Yeah."

"Okay, now. One, two, three . . . good. Terrific. Ten, eleven, watch out, twelve. Now we're on the sidewalk. Your stick probably rolled onto the side here, the pavement slants a little bit, feel it?"

"Uh . . . oh, yeah."

"Wait a minute." He stood there waiting while she tapped the walkway with her stick, and in a moment she had found the one that had got away from him.

"Here it is," she said, stooping to pick it up. She held it out to him, but he didn't know it. "Reach out your hand," She said. He took the stick from her. "Wrap the strap around your wrist, that's what it's for," she said.

She put her hand lightly through his arm and they started down the walk. She moved her stick skillfully in front of her, cutting a swath no wider than her own body, and it skimmed the walk just millimeters above the ground. But his was banging loudly and swinging too far from side to side; he tried to adjust it so it wouldn't make that awful tapping sound, but it was a tricky problem in gauging distance.

"You really can't see a thing?" she asked

him as they walked.

"No. Just blackness," he said.

"How do you feel?"

"Scared!"

She laughed and patted his arm reassuringly. All of a sudden he felt a whole rush of tossing, complicated emotions. Gratitude to her, for understanding and being so helpful; terror at what might happen to himself without the eyes he had always taken for granted; an odd kind of closeness to another human being he'd never experienced before, a sharing. Lots of things, all mixed up together. Apprehension, a sense of exhileration, daring and bold. He decided he didn't even care what other people would think if they saw him.

"Want to walk to the park?" she suggested.

"Sure."

"Or take the bus?"

"Uh . . . walk, if that's okay with you."

"Sure, I'd always rather walk. Anyway, I don't think you're prepared to deal with the kindness of strangers quite yet."

"What do you mean?"

"Watch out, you're veering to the left. Just relax, okay? What I mean is, everyone is so nice to you when you're blind. On a bus, the driver is usually very helpful in a very loud voice, and sometimes he even stops the bus till you find a seat, and people move over, and

. . . I'd rather walk. Not that I don't like people — I do, and I'm glad they're so nice, of course. But . . ."

"Yeah. I think I understand that part of it. Being the center of attention."

"Here's the curb. We'd better wait a minute before we cross. Listen for the traffic."

"There's a truck coming."

"Right. He's slowing down, though. Couple of other cars. They're stopping. Come on."

"Hey, are you sure? Maybe they're just being nice. There might be someone coming who doesn't see us. How do you know the light is green?"

"Come on, Jeff. The worst thing you can do is hesitate when you're crossing; people won't know which way you're going."

She led him firmly across the intersection and up the giant step which was the curb at the other side. He was sweating heavily, scared.

"The blind leading the blind," Eileen giggled. "Come on, you're safe with me."

"I guess you think I'm an awful idiot," he said.

"I think you're nice," she answered. "Blind, but nice."

Laughing, they strolled into the park, and Eileen led the way to the zoo area. She knew every turn and corner and pathway there.

Something moaned, or growled, or snorted

113

loudly very near them. Jeff jumped, startled. "What's that?"

"A bear," she said calmly.

"How can you tell?

She thought about that and answered, "Well, he smells like a bear. Take a deep breath. Bear, right?"

The bear growled again. Now that he knew what it was, he wondered how he'd ever been frightened by it.

"What does a bear smell like?" he mused, sniffing the air.

"Like . . . like a *bear*!"

"Oh. I guess everything has a smell, huh?"

"Sure. Most things."

"Do I?

"Do you what?"

"Do I have a smell?"

"Yes," she answered. He knew she was grinning, and he smiled a little tentatively.

"What do I smell like?" he ventured.

"Like . . . like a Jeff!"

He frowned. What was that supposed to mean?

"Hey, silly. I'm only teasing you."

A little uncomfortable with this subject, he turned away from the bear cage and started walking again.

"Apes," he said as they came up along the next series of animals.

"Terrific. How'd you know? By the smell?"

"No. They're talking. Hear them?"

"Sure. Chatter chatter chatter. Like the kids at school!"

"Anyway," he confessed, "I remembered that the monkey cage was right next to the bears."

"Good for you. Memory is the most important thing."

"Yeah, I guess it must be. Never thought of that before."

"You're learning a lot today," she said, laughing. "Let's go this way."

She turned off the zoo path toward the tunnel that led to the center of the park. Jeff came along obediently, but just inside the entrance to the tunnel he suddenly stopped.

"What's wrong?" she asked.

"I don't know. . . . I feel . . . strange. Disoriented . . . everything is black and . . . where are we?"

"In the tunnel," she said. "Hey, are you okay?"

He tried to cover it up, but he was overcome with dizziness and the weird sensation of echoes all around him. He was afraid to go on, afraid of entering a closed space. He knew the tunnel well, had never thought of it one way or another before; now it loomed menacing and strange. He felt pressures inside his head, and he heard the voices of other strollers, a child's whine, two men talking in booming, resounding, disembodied mutters. He couldn't find his balance, he thought he might fall down and never find the way to get back on his feet again.

"What is it, Jeff?" she asked, sounding worried.

"Oh . . . I'm not sure of anything like this. I feel like . . . like I'm in space or something. I'm afraid if I take a step, I'll fall a million miles. It's weird, Lee. . . . I'm scared."

"It's okay, Jeff. Honest," she said. Both her hands were on his arm now, trying to give him comfort, stability, reassurance.

"Do you ever feel like that?" he asked in a small voice.

"No," she said. "Come on, we can go back the other way, if you'd rather. We don't have to go through the tunnel."

"I think . . . maybe I should. Get over it. Come on." He forced himself to take a step forward, deeper into the tunnel. The feeling of vertigo stayed with him, but he held onto her arm and used his stick to feel the way. Each time he touched the ground in front of him he expected the stick to touch nothingness, and his feet were shuffling slowly, reluctant to leave the firm ground.

"Okay?" she asked. Her voice reverberated against the close walls of the enclosure, and all he could do was nod his head yes. She couldn't see him nod, but she understood. Slowly, they made their way through the tunnel and out into the sunshine.

"Let's find a bench and sit down for a

minute," she suggested. She led him slightly off toward the edge of the pathway, and expertly guided her stick in front of her at about knee level. It touched a bench, empty. "Here we are," she said, and they sat down.

Jeff was still perspiring, but the feeling of being scared and disoriented had been vanquished. At least for the moment.

"You okay?" she asked.

"Yes. I'm fine now. How come you never felt that way? I should think, not being able to see, that when your other senses get distorted like that, in a tunnel or . . . gosh, I should think it might happen in a lot of situations. Is that what happened when I threw you into the pool?"

"Hey, yeah, I guess so? I guess that's exactly what happened. I hadn't thought of it like that before. I never had that sensation in the tunnel, anyway. Or if I ever did, it must have been when I was a baby and I got over it. You do get over it. You get your confidence."

"How long does that take, I wonder?"

"Here comes the popcorn man. Hear him?"

Jeff listened, but he couldn't hear the whistle. "No," he said, "but I'm sure I will, in a minute."

them from what seemed a long way off. "Want some?" he asked her.

Sure enough, there it was, coming toward

"No, thanks. Not now. You go ahead, if you want to."

"Is it true that your other senses get keener when you lose the use of one?"

"Oh. I don't think so," she said. "People ask me that. I think what happens is just that you learn to use the other senses better. You rely on them more. I've had a lot more practice than you, Jeff. This is your first day. I've been blind all my life."

"Yeah," he murmured. That was something he really couldn't imagine. What was it like *never* to have seen anything?

"It's harder for people who lose their sight," she said thoughtfully. "They are more scared. I've never known anything different, so I don't mind it so much. Don't know what I'm missing, I suppose!" She tried to make a joke out of it.

"You mean . . . maybe you're not so wonderful as I'm beginning to think you are?" he said, pretending to be disappointed, and they both leaned back against the bench for a good laugh.

"Hey, did anybody ever hear you make a joke before?" she asked him.

"I don't think so," he answered. "I think my sense of humor is getting sharper, now that I can't see."

"Well, if you have to pick one of the senses," she said, laughing, "I think that's the one you'll need the most!"

CHAPTER 9

They walked some more in the park, and Jeff had the curious experience of listening to a softball game. It was almost as much fun as watching it, trying to picture what was happening from the shouts of the crowd and picking out the moment when the pitcher was winding up, when the bat swung and missed, or contacted the ball with a satisfying "thunk" that could be heard across the width of the grassy field.

"Want to find out the score?" Eileen asked him.

"How do you do that?"

She giggled. "Ask somebody," she answered.

"Clever," he commented.

"Well sometimes you have to."

"Do you want to know the score?"

"No," she said.

"Neither do I. How about something to eat? I'm suddenly starving."

"Good idea. There's usually a hot dog man over near home plate. Come on."

They made their way through the crowd watching the ballgame. People saw them coming, with their two canes, arm in arm, and made a path for them. Jeff nearly got caught up in the leash between a large dog and its master, but Eileen let him know with pressure on his arm that they should wait, just stand there and wait until the dog and owner untangled themselves. The man was murmuring apologies.

"That's okay," Eileen said cheerfully. "Can I pet your dog?"

"He bites," the man said.

She laughed, and they moved on. "People are strange," she commented. "Nice, but strange."

"I smell sauerkraut," Jeff said, sniffing the air.

"Dis must be de place," she said. They waited their turn at the busy hot dog stand, and soon they were juggling soda cans and franks, dripping sauerkraut. Eileen handled hers with practiced ease, but Jeff was having difficulty holding the food, his stick, and her arm all at the same time.

"Let's sit on the grass," she suggested, and led him off the path onto a little slope where they sat down for a mini-picnic.

Jeff was still holding the change from the bills he had given the vendor. He set the soda and paper plate down on the grass and held out his palm with the two quarters and dime on it.

"Do people cheat you with change and stuff?" he asked. He was trying to remember exactly how much franks and sodas were supposed to cost, but he'd never paid that much attention before.

"No," she answered. "I always know how much I'm giving, because I keep my bills separate, fold them differently. Look . . . oh, I forgot! You can't see. Well, what I do is this. I fold the fives in half, and the tens lengthwise. I don't fold the singles at all. Anything bigger than a ten, well, so far I haven't had to worry about that!"

"You'll think of a way, when the problem comes up," he said.

She heard the admiration in his voice, and found herself glad he couldn't see; her face was flushed. Quickly, she denied any credit for the scheme. "People teach you those things," she said. "I didn't exactly invent any of it."

121

"I guess you can tell the difference in change just by feeling the coins," he said.

"Right."

"Anyway," she said, "I think most people are honest. Don't you?"

"I . . . I guess so."

They munched on their hot dogs in contented silence for a little while. Jeff had some trouble with the sauerkraut dripping all over, and wished he had ordered his without. But you couldn't go through life doing without things, you had to learn to handle it.

"I guess I'm a pretty positive person," Eileen mused out loud. "I think people are honest, and kind, and life is great. I'm going to enjoy it. Every minute of it."

"That's terrific," he said with heartfelt sincerity.

She started to giggle.

"What's so funny?"

"At this place for the blind where I trained, they also train sighted people, like Mrs. Hays, you know. That's where I met her. Anyway, those people have to go around for a while like you are, with patches over their eyes and dark goggles and white canes. They have an awful time! Once I went out with this man, a young teacher, and we had lunch, and he asked me to order for both of us."

"Yeah?"

She giggled again. "I ordered spaghetti for

him. Wow . . . what a time he had with that stuff! It was sliding all over the place!"

"You're mean," Jeff said amiably. "You know that?"

She laughed out loud. "Yes, I know!"

He grinned as he crumpled his paper napkin and plate in both hands. "Like . . . I've probably got mustard and sauerkraut all over me right now."

She laughed. "I'll tell you what — we'll get you a bib!"

He reached out his hand to her. "Give me your garbage," he said. She put her crumpled up things in his hand. "I'll find a trash can," he said boldly. He stood up and waggled his stick in front of him, took a few steps, and found it. He felt with his hand to make sure, and dumped the papers and cans into the can. He felt an enormous sense of achievement. Another thing he'd taken for granted all his life; amazing how little things could suddenly get to be important. Imagine feeling like you'd really accomplished something, just for finding a garbage can all by yourself.

"Want to go back through the zoo?" she asked, putting her arm through his again.

"Sure."

"Come on, then. Back this way, right?" He was feeling pretty sure of himself now.

"You don't mind going through the tunnel again?"

"I'll be okay this time."

But it threw him. Sounds bouncing off the walls, the ceiling, no edges to anything, echoes and resonances he couldn't place, the sense of darkness closing in all around, the absence of the sun's warming benevolence. He clung to the idea that he'd be all right again as soon as he got into the sun. He wasn't even aware that he was clutching her arm tightly and breaking out into a sweat again. He forced one foot in front of the other, forced his stick to swing slowly in the same rhythm with hers, forced himself to keep his head up, and he was okay, almost.

There was one terrible instant. A little kid must have thrown a ball inside the tunnel; the sound of its bouncing and rolling reverberated eerily and Jeff started.

"It's a ball rolling," Eileen said very softly to him, and he knew that she had felt his whole body tense up. There wasn't very much you could hide from her.

"I'm okay," he murmured. "Thanks."

They were out of the tunnel.

"Sometimes there are sounds and noises you can't identify right away," she said, "but generally, there's nothing to be nervous about, except traffic, of course. And bicycles. Unless you're on them. Gee, too bad we can't go riding again today."

"How come you weren't nervous about

that?" he asked. "I think if I got on the back of a bike now and someone else was steering I'd be scared to death."

"You have to trust people," she said. "Okay?"

That meant she had trusted him. And in his ignorance he had almost killed them both. Well, anyway, he had been reckless up to a point. He just hadn't realized, then, that she trusted him absolutely with her life.

There was an awful lot to learn.

"Want to go to the bird house?" she asked when they came to the crossroads at the zoo area.

"Sure. If you do."

"Oh, I love the birds. I'm sorry they have to be in a cage, but the cage is enormous and they have plenty of room to fly around in. They sound happy enough, I guess."

But when they got there, Jeff was unprepared for the cacophony of sounds. Raucous yelps and trills and caws and shrieks and what sounded like someone screaming for help. It was horrible.

"What's wrong with them? What are they doing?" he asked her.

She caught the underlying panic in his voice and answered quickly, although she didn't understand why these normal sounds should upset him. "Nothing special," she said. "They always sound like that."

"I guess I never really listened before. It's awful, Lee. Sounds like ... did you ever see that Hitchcock movie about birds attacking people?"

"Yeah, I saw it."

"You go to movies?"

"Of course I do."

"Hey, can we get out of here, it's really spooky. I never realized it before, there are so many of them, all hollering at once, awful!"

"Sure. Let's keep on walking. Come on."

They hurried past the bird houses, and Jeff started to calm down again as the sounds receded behind them.

"It's funny. . . . I guess the colors and shapes of the birds get in your way of hearing them or something. But it really came as a shock, hearing all that noise all of a sudden."

"Hi, Lee!" Someone greeted her, a boy's voice, not more than a few feet away.

"Oh, hi, Paul. How're you doin'?"

"Fine, great . . . uh . . . see you."

"See you, Paul."

"Who was that?" Jeff asked.

"Oh, just a guy from school."

"Oh."

He was thinking about people seeing you, and you not being able to see them. He wondered if anybody from his own school was around today in the park, seeing him, thinking he was off his rocker completely, and not saying anything to let him know they were even there. The automatic flush of self-consciousness didn't have much time to build in him, though. He found himself thinking "that's their problem, if my being blind makes them uptight," and something like a huge clean wave of fresh air seemed to go through him, incredibly pleasant. Free.

Something about that made him appreciate Eileen even more, and he was really glad to be with her. He sniffed the air hard, trying to figure out where they were now. He was all turned around, and couldn't remember what came after the bird house in the zoo. He'd been there a million times in his life, but he'd always relied on his eyes to mark the familiar paths.

She was very sure-footed and led him easily, strolling along as if there were a map in her head, which of course there was.

"Would you excuse me a minute?" she asked. "I promised to call my mom. Here's the phone booth, it'll just take a minute."

They stopped, and he lifted his stick to probe ahead of him. It touched the side of the phone booth.

"That's terrific," he said.

"Elementary, my dear Watson," she said. She took her hand from his arm and moved away. He heard the door of the booth creak

127

as she entered, and then it closed. He was standing alone, trying not to keep touching the side of the phone booth as if he needed support. Even keeping your balance was something you had to learn.

He heard her dialing, dimly. Casually, he crossed his arms and leaned against the phone booth, waiting. He set a little smile on his face, in case . . . in case of what, he wasn't quite sure.

He listened to the sounds around him. Voices murmuring nearby, shouting in the distance, kids crying, and people talking in serious low tones as they strolled past. A dog yelped, and he heard something running toward him. Scratching sounds, or large claws on the sidewalk, running toward him, something . . . the dog. It yelped and then barked, very close by.

Jeff jumped inside his skin. The dog was yapping at his feet, really barking ferociously, and threatening to attack him. Where was the owner? The dog sounded vicious, and Jeff had no protection against it.

"Go 'way," he whispered, and repeated it again and again, louder and louder. "Go 'way, go away!"

This seemed only to excite the dog, whose bark became more threatening. Jeff's instinct was to thrash out with his stick, but he had never hurt a living thing before, even in self-defense. He wouldn't strike out at the dog until it bit him or something. Where in hell was the owner? There was a leash law in this city, people ought to be aware that their pets could attack and even kill someone who couldn't protect himself, a blind person was helpless against a killer dog.

The barking was louder and faster, and Jeff backed away from the phone booth, off into space he couldn't judge. "Leave me alone!" he said fiercely to the dog. He didn't want to shout, to call attention to himself, even at the risk of being crunched by those great teeth he was imagining; somehow being the center of attention was worse than being bitten by a mad dog. "Get out of here, go away!" he urged the dog desperately. He was terrified.

He moved his stick in front of him, trying to poke the dog, to push him away without actually striking him. The dog only got more excited, and the barking got louder, and the growls between barks grew ominous, and he knew the animal was ready to sink its teeth into his leg.

He hit the phone booth with the stick and leaped toward it. He wrenched the door open and crowded inside with Eileen.

"Okay, Mom," she was saying. "So long." She hung up the receiver and turned to him in the crowded space. He had wedged himself inside. He was trying to shut the door, and she could feel his whole body trembling.

"What's the matter?" she asked, alarmed.

"There's a dog outside . . . ferocious . . ." he said breathlessly.

"Really? My gosh!"

"He attacked me," Jeff said. He had got the door shut and they were standing inside the glass enclosure, safe for the moment, and huddled together in the tiny space. Jeff was gasping, trying to catch his breath.

They heard the dog bark once outside the booth, and then the voice of its owner coming over to capture the beast.

"Here, Fluffy, come on back," the man cooed.

"Fluffy?" Eileen echoed. Her voice had a definite trace of amusement in it. More than a trace.

Jeff said nothing, still trying to breathe normally after the close escape.

"Funny name for a vicious killer dog," Eileen mused aloud.

"I don't care what his name is. He's a menace," Jeff said firmly.

Fluffy yelped once more outside the phone booth where they waited, and they heard his owner talking a kind of baby-talk to him as he led the dog away.

"Want a biscuit, naughty pup? Come on, up on my lap, and have your snick-snack, Fluff.

Neither Eileen nor Jeff said anything for a

moment, and he had the uncomfortable feeling she was trying to keep from laughing. But she was quiet, and they listened until it was clear that the man and his dog had gone away.

"I think it's safe now," she said.

"Yeah. I guess so," he answered. He did feel a little sheepish, and grateful to her for not laughing. The uncomfortable image flashed through his head of what Fluffy probably really looked like. Well, if it was a small dog, it sure had a large bark, anyway.

They walked out of the booth and away from the zoo area, along the perimeter of the park.

"Hey . . . wait a minute," Jeff said, stopping to listen.

"What?"

"Listen."

The tinkle of the bell on the ice cream man's wagon was singing about the yammer of the people in the park. It was a bright, happy, melodious sound, soaring over the background clatter and chatter and shouting, a single crystal-clear note . . . no, two notes, three . . . it was music.

"What is it? Eileen asked, puzzled.

"Shhh . . . my gosh, don't you hear it?"

"What? Oh, you mean the ice cream man's bell?"

"It's so beautiful."

Clear and sweet, the bell sang out with

humor and a lyrical jauntiness of its own, and nobody was listening to it. Not even Eileen.

"What a nice sound," he said. "I never noticed it before."

"Yeah," she agreed. She still sounded a little puzzled, and maybe kind of impatient, too.

"But you must hear it all the time," he said. "You must hear things like that, that other people don't bother to listen to."

"Well," she said slowly, thoughtfully, "I guess I don't listen as much as you think. I mean, I guess I don't hear things the way you're doing right now. It's your first time. I'm used to it, like anybody else, I guess."

"It's amazing," he said, as they started to walk again. "I'm really hearing things, today. Little dogs sound big, and voices in a tunnel make me lose my balance, and the ice cream bell sounds like . . . it's beautiful," he finished lamely.

"Yes," she said, "it really is. You're making *me* listen, too."

"Hey," he laughed, "how about that?"

"Now what do your hear?" she asked him.

The ice cream bell had faded off in the distance behind them, and now there was the unmistakable jangle of the carousel off to their left.

"I hear it," he said, "but it doesn't turn me on as much as the little bell did."

"Want a ride?" she suggested.

"Sure!"

They made their way to the carousel, where the smell of popcorn and cotton candy and the excited shouts of the little kids competed with the loud presence of the clanging calliope music.

"Is it going?" he asked her.

"No, it's stopped. Come on, let's get on."

They used their sticks to edge up onto the high turntable platform, and found two horses side by side.

"How'd you know it was stopped?" he asked curiously as they began to mount the steeds.

"Long years of experience," she said. "It creaks when it's going and you can usually feel the rush of wind when the thing really starts to go and you're standing close enough. And anyway, there are always lots of shouts, the little kids hollering 'hi Mom' and 'look at me!'"

"You okay?" he asked her. She was already seated high on the outside horse, but he was having a little problem finding the stirrup to set his foot into.

"Hey . . . you kids!"

It was the rough, growly voice of the man who ran the carousel. He was on the turntable, coming toward them from the center where the mechanical works were. Was he talking to them?

"How much?" Jeff asked, turning in the direction of the man's gruff voice. "For two?"

He found the stirrup, set his sneaker solidly inside it, grabbed the smooth metal pole, and hoisted himself onto the horse. The stick hung from his wrist by its strap. He dug into his pocket with the other hand to reach his wallet.

"No way," the man said. "You'll have to get off."

"Huh? Why?" Jeff asked.

"Come on. Both of you. Don't give me any trouble, okay?"

"Trouble! We just want to ride. I asked you how much for the tickets, that's all."

"Listen . . . I said you'll have to get off. Come on, now, I got to start this thing up."

Jeff gripped the pole with his fist. His knuckles turned white from the anger that was beginning to fill him. He knew people must be staring at them. Why was this man making a scene? What was happening.

"I don't know what you mean," he said.

"I can't take you people, that's all. Now come on, like a good kid. Don't make trouble."

"Come on, Jeff," Eileen said quietly. She began to dismount, and he felt her hand reaching up to tug at his arm gently.

"What people?" Jeff persisted angrily. "We just want to ride. I don't understand."

"You ain't allowed," the man said. "I can't have blind people on the horses."

"Please, Jeff, it's all right. Come on," Eileen urged him in a very low voice.

"What's wrong with blind people?" Jeff insisted, holding onto the pole more tightly than before. His hand was making a fist that wanted to break something.

"I don't have insurance for your kind," the man said. "I ain't covered."

"But I've been on this a million times," he said. He had started to ask Eileen, hadn't she said she'd been on the carousel before? But he had stopped himself and turned the question around. "I've ridden this thing all my life," he repeated.

"Not with me here, buddy. Look, I don't want to be mean or nothing, but you got to go. Come on."

Jeff felt the man's hand on his arm, pulling him. Eileen had moved back, and he could only sense her there, standing and waiting, hating the scene he was making.

"Take your hands off me!" he shouted furiously at the man.

"Please, Jeff, come on. It's okay," she said from a few feet away.

"That's right, lady, thanks," the man muttered. "Come on, kid, I'll help you down. My customers want to ride."

"We're customers," Jeff heard himself insisting. "We just want a crummy ride, that's all."

"Hey, Mister," a child's voice piped up from the horse behind him. "Let's go!"

"Giddyap," another child's voice rang out nearby.

"Come on, Jeff," Eileen said again. He knew that she was embarrassed, and for her sake he loosened his hold on the pole and began to slide off the horse.

"Okay, Lee," he said. For her sake. . . . He didn't know whether the man was still standing there or had moved off. He didn't know how many people were watching them curiously as they tapped with their sticks to find their way off the turntable. Eileen took his arm again and they stood a few feet back as the horses began to move and the calliope music seemed to rise to a frantic pace.

"You're right," he muttered, "you *can* tell when it's moving."

"Oh, Jeff, don't be upset. It happens sometimes, that all. There are some people who just don't understand."

"It's terrible!" he said.

"It's probably not his fault. He isn't insured for blind people," she said with a sigh. "Don't blame him."

"How do you stand it? It's awful!"

"Oh, who cares about a silly ride anyway? It's for kids."

They walked away from the shouting and laughing and the gross, wheezing music.

"I thought you said you'd been on it before?" he asked her casually.

"Oh, sure. With my parents, or my sister, or somebody like that. I guess it's okay if you're with a sighted person."

"Oh."

It sounded to him as if people assumed that blind people were feeble-minded or something, as if they couldn't take care of themselves. Had he been guilty of thinking that, ever?

"I know what," she said. "Let's cross over to the other side of the street. There's another little park there, do you know it?"

"Uh . . . I'm not sure."

"It's just a sort of empty lot, really. but there are flowers and it's peaceful. Not very many people. It's right across this intersection."

"Lee . . ."

"Hm?"

"Did I ever act like that? You know, like that guy?"

"Like the man on the carousel?"

"Yeah."

"Of course not! I'm not sure I know what you mean."

"Oh . . . well . . . I'm not sure I do, either, come to think of it."

They were laughing as they left the crowded park, and they weren't even sure why.

CHAPTER 10

Still shaken from his encounter with the carousel man and the unexpected force of his own anger rising in him, Jeff was not thinking about keeping his other senses alert.

"Here's the curb," Eileen warned him.

He stepped down and would have continued walking, but she held him back with slight pressure on his arm.

"Hey, wait a minute," she said. "The light's red for us."

The cars were whizzing past. He felt like a real idiot. He stepped back and waited with her.

"There! Hear that?" she said.

"What? The cars?"

"Under the noise of the traffic. The signal light. It just changed to orange. Didn't you hear it click?"

"No," he admitted.

"Ten seconds, then it'll turn green. I guess It's just something you have to get used to listening for. Some corners have it and some don't."

The cars were slowing now and he heard a screech of brakes. He listened for the clicking of the traffic light, but wasn't at all sure he heard anything. She took a step forward.

"It's green now," she said. "Come on."

She stepped briskly, but Jeff was suddenly terrified to walk in front of all those cars and trucks. What if she was wrong; what if it took too long for them to cross; what if some of the drivers didn't see them. He found his feet strangely heavy and could hardly move.

"Let's go," Eileen said. "We don't have much time."

She was almost pulling him along, right out Into the middle of the street, that busy intersection where impatient drivers, thinking about getting home or beating the next light, might just pull ahead, thinking that the two blind kids had the reactions of normal people, that they could see and jump out of the way. He stopped in his tracks. He could feel the closeness of a car's engine, hear the motor revving up, ready to plow ahead. The cars suddenly loomed all around them; he could hear the traffic going across in the other direction. Nobody stopped to see what was in their paths, nobody looked.

"Hurry up, Jeff," she said. "The light's going to change again."

That didn't help. He really froze now. He couldn't move his feet at all. He was standing right in the middle of the street, and she was tugging at his arm. A car honked its horn impatiently; Jeff jumped back.

"What's that?"

"It's okay," she said. "Come on."

Suddenly, there was a loud clicking sound.

"Did you hear that?" Jeff screamed. "It's orange! The light is changing! Where are we? Halfway?"

He stumbled, and in his struggle to regain his balance, he shoved her away from him.

"Jeff!"

"They won't wait!" he shouted. "Where are you? The cars won't wait for us!"

She reached out and took his arm firmly. "Yes, they will," she said. "But you can't go back. You can't just stand here. Now, come on!"

There was another click. Somehow the sounds of the street and honking of the cars faded into the distance and all he could hear was the thunderous sound of the traffic signal clicking as the light changed from green to red.

"It's green!"

Motors were revving now, and more horns blasting at them, and he heard one car on the far side of the street whiz right by. Now they would all go; they wouldn't wait; they wouldn't see them. The two of them, exposed and helpless, caught in the middle of the street, small specks in the way of those cars. He panicked and fell to his knees. His legs just refused to support him suddenly, and now the cars in other lanes began to move past them on both sides.

"No! No! Wait!" he shouted frantically, reaching up his hand to signal the traffic to stop. But he was down so low he couldn't be seen. Horns and accelerators and shouting, angry drivers built up a force on the other side of his unseeing blank wall. He was alone and they were going to drive right over him.

"Jeff!" Eileen sounded far away now. Had she gone ahead and crossed the street? Was she calling to him from the other side, safe? Had she left him here to be run over in his panic? The cars whizzed by him on both sides.

"Jeff!"

"Lee . . ." Somehow, he found the strength to get to his feet again, and a car swerved so close he could feel its horrible, hot mechanical breath on his legs as the exhaust swept by him. "Wait! Wait!" he called out to the cars, but they were gunning along, oblivious of him, their target, standing alone and blind in the middle of the death trap.

His hands reached up and began to tear at the tape that covered his eyes. The sunglasses had hit the pavement and been crushed by unseeing radial tires, for sure. There was only the tape, the blackness between him and safety. He had to get it off, had to see, to save himself.

"What are you doing?" Eileen cried, very close to him now. She found his arm again and held it tightly. She wasn't trying to pull him along now; it was too late for that. She hadn't left him alone, after all . . . that had only been an illusion. She had stayed right by him, right in the middle of the traffic, instead of saving herself.

"What are you doing?" she asked again.

He was clawing at his face. "Taking this junk off!" he screamed.

"No!" she ordered, and the tone of her voice was firm, so firm that he automatically turned to her, let his hands fall down from his face and stood there helplessly, waiting for her to tell him what to do.

"Now come with me," she said. She led him forward slowly, and he walked with her. He could hear the cars stopping, heard the brakes slammed on and gears grinding. His stick was dragging after them, but hers was held high, waved at waist-height ahead of her, signaling the oncoming cars and being obeyed. They made it to the opposite curb.

"Step up," she said, and he did.

"We're all right now," she assured him. "Take it easy."

"I'm sorry," he said. "I panicked."

"That's okay," she answered. "Just rest for a minute. Get your breath."

It was true, he was gasping for breath. She, too, was breathing deeply; of course, it had been a real fright for her, too. He had nearly got them both killed.

"What a coward I am," he muttered. "I'm sorry."

"It's okay."

"No, really . . . my God, Lee . . . How do you do it?"

"Well, for one thing, once you start across the street, you keep on going. You have to, otherwise the cars don't know what to expect."

"Yeah."

"You get used to it," she said.

"Do you *really*?" he asked her.

"Hey, you're not a coward. Perfectly normal reaction."

"I think you're . . ."

"What?" she asked when it seemed he wasn't going to finish his sentence.

"Well . . . I think you're terrific," he said.

"Why? Cause I know how to get across the street?" She laughed, and made it all right again.

"I just never realized a lot of things," he said.

"Feel okay now?"

"Yes."

"The park is just over this way." She put her hand in his hand, instead of through his arm. It felt good, even though he was conscious of the fact that his palms were sticky and moist. He held her hand gratefully, and they walked the few steps to the little triangle of greenery where flowers had been planted between the bushes.

"Bench or grass?" she asked.

"Uh . . . grass."

"Here, there's an opening here between this bush and the first bench. Follow me."

She led him onto a flat grassy area, and they sat down.

"Nice, huh?" she said.

"Yeah. No people."

"They're all around us, but somehow they don't hang around here. They all seem to go over to the big park instead. I love this place."

"It smells good."

"Yes. Fresh grass and lots of flowers. There are bushes over there. In May they have lilacs on them and they smell the sweetest of anything. I guess it won't be long before they're covered with snow."

"Something's blooming now, do you smell it?"

"Yes. Nearby."

"Very nearby," he agreed, inhaling deeply. She was moving around.

"What're you doing?" he asked.

"Sneaking up on the flowers. I just have to feel one. Oh, here. Here it is. Oh, Jeff . . . feel how smooth and soft. . . ."

He followed the sound of her voice and held out his hand. His fingers touched hers again, and then he touched the flower petals.

"They're silky," he said. It was strange and and incredibly delicate against his finger. He'd always looked at flowers before and smelled them, of course, but he couldn't remember whether he'd ever touched the petals of one before. Not without looking at it first, that was for sure. It was as if he'd never known that flowers were alive, really, with their own skin and it almost felt like it was breathing. He felt an awe for the incredible beauty of it.

"What kind are they?" she asked him.

"I don't know."

"They're so beautiful. I've got to know," she said softly.

"I could ask somebody," he said. But they listened for a moment, and there was no one around.

"Who?" she asked.

"I don't know. We're alone, I think."

"Yes, we are. You and I and this beautiful flower, maybe lots of beautiful flowers."

He reached toward the flower again. His fingers touched her hand again. It was almost as soft as the flower, but warmer and even nicer.

"Jeff?"

"Yeah."

"Do me a favor?"

"Sure."

She waited a minute before she asked. It was enough time for him to let his mind go kind of free and hopeful, wondering what favor he could do, if it had anything to do with their being alone, with their hands touching.

"Take that stuff off your eyes?" she asked him quietly.

"Now?"

"Yes."

He hesitated.

"Please," she said.

"Okay." He started to peel off the tape. She sat on the grass as motionless as a statue.

"Just a sec," he said. He pulled at the tape, which came away reluctantly, as if the darkness of it were part of him. He kept his eyes tightly shut; they felt vulnerable, shocked by the hot glare of sunlight pounding at his exposed lids.

He opened his eyes. An involuntary cry escaped his lips, but he wasn't aware of it. The blinding flash of color almost knocked him over. Green, green everywhere — the different greens of the grass, the leaves on the trees and the variegated bushes. Brilliant and soft, shimmering with the sun and darkening in the shadows. And the sky, bluer than he ever remembered it, with one white cloud floating miraculously up there over her head.

Her hair was filled with light, the long darkish strands framed her creamy skin and round red mouth, her clear blue eyes that smiled at him. She was wearing a plaid blouse with a blue sweater. Her hand was still touching the flower, whose petals were the most incredibly lovely shade of yellow he had ever seen. He felt as if he had never seen yellow at all before, or blue or green. Or anything. He looked at her and around them both at the world, blazing with light and color.

"Tell me," she said softly. She was cradling the flower in her hand.

"Well," he said, "they're yellow . . . and there's a lot of them, they're spread all over the grass here, I guess they must grow wild. Let's see . . . they have five or six petals each, and . . . and a reddish thing in the center, with fluffy stuff on it. . . . They're beautiful."

"Yes," she murmured. She was smiling.

"Everything's beautiful," he said, looking around. "The sky, the trees, the grass, the colors are fantastic." He laughed with sheer joy at it all. "Hey, you know," he said, "it's like a fairy tale. I never realized . . . look, Lee."

He cut himself off short. He hadn't learned a thing. Here he was, telling her to *look*.

She could never take off the blinders and have the rush of color and light and gratitude for its all being there. She could never see any of it, never. She never had and she never would.

"I'm sorry," he whispered.

She reached out her hand to touch his. "It's okay, Jeff," she said softly, and he knew she really meant it. "I can feel how nice it is from your voice."

"You can?"

"Yes."

"I wish . . ."

"I don't," she said. "I don't wish. It's a waste of energy. I'd rather spend all my wishing energy on listening, and feeling, and imagining. I can see how beautiful everything is, if you share it with me like you're doing."

They were very quiet for a long time then, and just sat holding hands, with the grass

under them, and the sun, and the nice feeling.
Jeff looked around at everything, still with
a kind of astonishment at it all, but his glance
kept returning to Eileen's face. He thought
what a wonderful thing a human being was.
There was so much life in her; she generated
more warmth and light than the sun on the
grass or the scattered yellow flowers all
around them.

"You know what's beautiful?" he heard
himself saying.

"What?"

"*You're* beautiful," he said.

She didn't say anything at first, but he
didn't worry about having said the wrong
thing. It had come out so naturally, so easy,
and he meant it so much that he knew she
would have to believe him and be glad.

Finally, she said, a little shaky, trying to be
casual, "You mean it?"

"I mean it."

"I . . . I've always had trouble with that
one," she said, with a wistful smile. "I've
never really understood, about looks. My own
looks, especially. But . . ."

"But what?"

"But I believe you," she said. Her smile
wasn't wistful now, but happy, and Jeff felt
happy, too.

"Wait a minute," he said. He scrambled to
his feet and went over to one of the brightest,

tallest of the yellow flowers. He knelt down to it.

"What are you doing?" she asked him.

"I'm taking one of these flowers," he answered from a few feet away. "I know it's against the law, but I think they'll forgive me just this once."

He came back to her and put the flower in her hand.

"Here," he said.

She took the offering and bent her head down to inhale its sweetness. Her hands held the flower lovingly, and when she looked up toward him again she was glowing with some of the blossom's own reflected light against her skin.

"Perfume!" she exclaimed.

"Yeah. . . ."

"Thank you, Jeff."

Instead of sitting back down beside her, he stood there, suddenly awkward again.

"I guess we ought to start for home pretty soon," he said. "It's getting late."

"Okay," she said with her usual cheerfulness. "It's been a lovely Sunday." She got up from the grass, brushed the back of her jeans, and touched the flower to her nose briefly once more. She wrapped the strap of her stick around her wrist and was ready to go.

"Take my arm?" he said.

Eileen grinned, and then she quickly folded her stick. She put it away in her shoulder bag and reached out toward him.

"Sure," she said. "I almost forgot. You don't need me to show you the way any more."

When they came to the intersection at the edge of the little secluded park, Jeff was surprised to see how ordinary the corner crossing was. It had loomed as wide as the Indianapolis Raceway, and now he recognized it as a normal street which he had crossed thousands of times before. The light was green and they walked across with plenty of time before the signals changed. He listened for the clicking noise of the signal indicator, and was pleased to note that he heard it loud and clear. He'd just never noticed it before; he was sure that after today's experience he would go through the rest of his life noticing lots of new things.

He was grateful to her for not saying anything about the last time they'd crossed this street.

"Hey, Lee," he said casually as they stepped up onto the opposite curb, "I just thought of something."

"What?"

"Well, I heard about this dance our two schools are having after the game next week. Have you heard about that?"

"Oh, yeah. It seems to me I did hear something about that," she said.

"Uh . . . want to go with me?"

"I'd like that," she said.

"Me, too," he grinned.

CHAPTER 11

"Hey, Larry, hi." Jeff ran to catch up with his classmate.

"Yeah, hi!" Larry answered. He slowed down to match his stride with Jeff's, wondering what happened to make this guy suddenly so friendly. He'd always seemed standoffish before.

"You going to the dance Saturday night?" Jeff asked casually. He hoped it was casual, anyway. He'd never done this kind of thing before, but he'd heard it plenty of times. All Larry could do was say no, right?

"Yeah, sure. Are you?"

"Yeah. Uh . . . are you doubling with anybody?"

"Sure. I'm taking Nell, and we're going with Hank and Sharon. Hank's got his dad's car."

"Oh. Uh . . . that's terrific. Well, I guess I'll see you there, then."

They walked up the steps and into the main hall without saying anything else. Larry was trying to figure out what Jeff wanted to say. Larry was not exactly quick, but he wasn't dumb either, and it finally dawned on him as they split to go in two different directions. He turned and called out after Jeff.

"Hey . . . Jeff?"

"Yeah?"

The kids swarmed between them, dashing to the first class of the morning. Larry's voice boomed down the hall toward Jeff.

"You want to come with us? I mean, there's room in the car, if you want to come with us. You got a date?"

"Sure! Great, Larry. Hey, thanks a lot!"

"Sure." He turned to go down the hall and stopped again to shout once more. "Hey, Jeff!"

"Yeah?"

"Who's your girl?"

"Woman," muttered a long-haired person in jeans as she hurried past him.

"Oh, you don't know her. She goes to Eastern. Name's Eileen."

"Oh, okay. See you."

"See you."

155

It wasn't so hard to talk to people, after all, he thought as he turned into his classroom. All you needed was something to talk about.

His dad was pleased and so was his mother. She'd begun to think he'd never start asking girls out. Nothing was said about Eileen's being blind, nothing at all. It just wasn't such a big deal any more.

Eileen and her sister went shopping together, and had a great time trying on practically every dress in the store. They finally picked out a pleated skirt and matching vest for Lucy, to wear with a white blouse, and Eileen found a simple one-piece dress with a swirly skirt made out of a fabric as soft as real silk.

"All I want to know is, would it go with a yellow flower?" she asked Lucy.

"Yellow flower? Is he going to give you yellow flowers? How do you know?"

"I don't. I just want a dress that would look pretty in case it had a yellow flower to go with it. Maybe in my hair?"

"Well, this would be terrific with a yellow flower. It's kind of reddish-orange, really pretty. If he doesn't bring you a flower, you could always take out that one you're drying in the dictionary and stick that in your hair. Dead, but not forgotten."

"Very funny. Come on, Lucy, I need your help. You sure?"

"Would I lie to you?"

"Reddish-orange, huh?"

"Yeah."

"Really pretty?"

"Honest, Lee. It's beautiful."

"Okay. I mean, I don't know what I'm getting so intense about. It's only an old dance."

"You like him, don't you?"

"Sure. He's nice."

Lucy sighed with exaggerated loudness in the little dressing room. "My little sister, going out on her very first date. I'd better keep an eye on you, I suppose."

"Don't you dare!"

Lucy laughed. "Well, I sure am dying to see this guy Jeff, I'll tell you that."

"Well," Eileen said, struggling out of the new dress and back into her jeans, "if you're good and mind your own business, I might let you have a dance with him. Just one."

"Let me get a look at him, first."

"What have looks got to do with it, anyway?" Eileen retorted.

"Well, you look so pretty in that dress, it would be a pity if Jeff turned out to be anything less than sensational."

"Oh, Lucy, it's only a school dance."

"Come on, I'll buy you a soda."

"Okay. Oh, on the way, I want you to help

me pick out a lipstick, something reddish-orange, maybe?"

"Sure. I guess I should get one, too."

"Yeah, blue, to match your dress!" Eileen laughed.

They tried on their new dresses for their mother, who confirmed Lucy's opinion that the colors were perfect, and made Eileen swing around as if she were dancing, to see how high the skirt flew up, just to be sure.

The game was a tie, which made everybody at both schools reasonably happy, if mildly frustrated. "Wait'll next year!" they were all shouting to each other as they filed out of the stadium.

"Wow, that was exciting!" Eileen said. "I think I'm a little hoarse from screaming so much."

"I really thought we had you there, till the last three minutes," Jeff said.

"You do the best running commentary of anybody," she went on. "Better than Howard Cosell. Better than my sister, that's for sure! She says things like . . . 'uh, I think that was a punt . . .' and it'll be long after the play is over." She was laughing, and her cheeks were red from the wind and the excitement. She looked terrific with red cheeks.

"Want another hot dog?" he asked her as

they moved out with the crowd to the street.

"No, thanks. I've had three already!"

"Well, I guess we should mosey on home, get ready for the dance tonight."

"Okay. You don't have to walk me home. I'll see you later."

"About eight-thirty?"

"Fine."

"Uh . . . you don't mind . . . that we're going with these other kids?"

"Mind? Of course not! It'll be lots more fun that way."

"Okay. Well . . . see you then."

"See you," she called out happily, and turned toward her house. He saw her reach for her stick, and suddenly he changed his mind and ran the few steps to catch up with her again.

"Listen, I might as well walk you home. I mean . . . I'd like to, okay?"

"Sure," she said. She put the stick back in her bag.

Other kids walking home from the game passed them and lots of them said "hi." Suddenly it seemed to Jeff that he had joined the human race. He had lots of friends. He even had a girl. Nobody stared at them. He found himself looking forward to the dance with tremendous pleasure and anticipation.

"I really like to dance," he said.

"Me, too."

"How's your hustle?" he asked her.

"Wait and see."

"Mine's fantastic."

She laughed with delight. "Hey . . . is your name Jeff?"

"Huh?"

"Is this the same shy boy who couldn't think of anything to say and would fall down in a faint if he tried to make a joke?"

"Oh, him. No, I left him back there someplace. He fell into a tunnel."

"Poor thing."

"Good riddance."

"Here's my house," she said. They stood for a minute, her arm linked through his, smiling at each other. Then she broke away and started up the steps with sure feet.

The only thing was, they didn't seem to be touching the concrete at all, to her. She seemed somehow to be kind of floating.

"See you later," she called out.

"Eight-thirty!"

"Okay."

She went into the house, and Jeff turned to go. He had a stop to make on the way home. There was a florist on the corner near his bus stop who had those yellow flowers in his window.

"It's beautiful!" she exclaimed when he handed it to her.

"Too big to wear in your hair," Lucy commented. "Hi, Jeff. I'm Lucy."

"Hi. I didn't mean for her to wear it. I mean, I just thought . . ."

"I'm going to put it in a vase," Eileen said. "I'll bet it lasts for days and days. Oh . . . Jeff, this is my mother."

"Hello, Jeff."

"Hello."

Outside, the car honked impatiently.

"Well, I guess we'd better go," Jeff said.

"Okay. Night, Mom."

"Have a good time, kids."

Out on the sidewalk, hurrying toward the car with all the others leaning out curiously to see them, Jeff was suddenly swept back into self-consciousness for a minute. Eileen seemed to sense this and spoke quickly to him, before they reached the others.

"Thanks for the yellow flower, Jeff."

"How'd you know it was yellow?"

"Am I right?"

"Sure."

She chuckled. His moment of discomfort passed. "Lee?"

"What?"

"You look terrific. I like that dress."

"Jeff?" She stopped him with a little tug on his arm just before they got to the car.

"What?"

"You look terrific, too."

161

Larry and Nell in the back seat made room for them; with some laughing and scrambling, Eileen finally ended up on Jeff's lap, and they were on their way. The introductions were made in the dark as the car moved toward the school, and by the time Hank found a parking place, they were all singing both school songs and laughing like old happy friends.

It was a wonderful evening, almost enchanted. Eileen had lots of partners; her laugh and nimble grace on the dance floor were contagious, and all the guys wanted to dance with her. Jeff danced with lots of other girls, too, but found himself always looking for her when the music stopped. It wasn't because he thought she couldn't find him, or take care of herself. It was because he wanted to be with her.

The music was wonderful. The decision to spend the money on getting the best possible group rather than on decorations was a wise one, everyone agreed. Who cared if the auditorium was a bit on the stark side? The seats had been taken out and the group sat up on the stage and the lights had been dimmed and it was transformed. It was the Palladium, the Kit Kat Klub, the Circus, Studio 54 . . . whatever you wanted it to be when you closed your eyes. Everyone agreed.

Afterwards, the six of them bundled into the car again and went for pizza all the way down at the far end of the city. They talked about the music and the game and the way people were dressed or not dressed, and who was surprisingly good on the dance floor, and what a super evening it had been.

When they piled out of the car and into the narrow little restaurant, they all agreed they were starving and ordered three jumbos with everything on them.

"Your lipstick's a little smeared, Lee," Sharon said as they settled into the wide booth. She was sitting across from Eileen, and dug into her purse to hand over a small round mirror. "Look. Just there, see?"

Eileen smiled. She didn't reach for the mirror.

"You'll have to show me." She leaned forward, toward Sharon. "Where?"

Sharon stared at her. Eileen's eyes were blue and clear and unseeing.

"I didn't know you were blind!" she blurted out.

The group froze. No one said anything. Then Eileen broke into giggles, and the others stirred uncomfortably, glancing at each other, not wanting to look at either Eileen or Sharon.

Jeff laughed easily and took Eileen's hand. "Hey," he said, "that's quite a statement, isn't it?"

"That might be the nicest thing anyone's ever said to me," Eileen agreed promptly.

"Oh, I'm so sorry!" Sharon said in a stricken voice.

"Oh, don't be! Don't you see? It's a compliment. Here we've spent a whole evening together and you didn't even know. I think that's terrific!"

"Don't be sorry, Sharon," Jeff said quietly. "It was an okay thing to say, honestly."

Eileen put out her hand in Sharon's direction, and the embarrassed girl took it. Everyone else stared at the two hands joined across the table.

"Friends?" Eileen said.

"Friends!" Sharon echoed.

"Friends! Friends!" the others chimed in, and the bubbly spirit of the group came back almost as strong as it had been before. But Jeff was aware of the little sidelong glances, of the ripple of tension that the others were feeling now. He remembered how it was when he had felt that way around Eileen. Way back in the dark ages.

He knew they were regarding him differently now, too. Why would a guy take out a blind girl? That's what Larry and Hank were probably thinking. They liked Eileen, he knew that, and they hadn't even noticed . . . but now that they knew, it was different. People were strange. He felt kind of sorry for them in their ignorance.

The pizzas came and were devoured eagerly

by all, and the jukebox was played until most of its selections had been tested, and the empty soda bottles were lined up along the table and it was time to go home.

Hank dropped Jeff and Eileen off at her house first; the others all lived on the west side of town. The girls acted like they lived on different planets and might never see each other again, althought they kept promising to call each other and get together often. Finally, all the "good nights" were said, and the car drove off, leaving Eileen and Jeff alone in the quiet darkness.

"I had a wonderful time," Eileen said.

"Me, too," Jeff agreed.

"I like your friends. I like . . . I liked the dance," she said.

They walked slowly toward the steps leading up to her house. It was very dark, except for the streetlight on the corner, and the dim bulb that threw a welcoming glow from the top of her front door. They walked up the steps very slowly, one at a time, stopping to talk after each riser.

"You were the hit of the dance," he said.

"Oh, sure. Belle of the ball, that's me."

"No, really."

They mounted another step.

"For an ordinary school dance, I thought it was pretty good," Jeff said.

"Do you go to a lot of them?"

He grinned. "That was my first," he admitted.

She laughed, too, and they took another step up.

"I hope your mom won't be angry. It's pretty late," he said.

"I guess she's probably waiting up."

"Yeah."

Another step, and then he couldn't think of anything to say except, "You really are beautiful, Lee."

"Hey, are you kidding? I know I've got pizza smeared all over my chin, it feels sticky. And my lipstick's probably long gone."

And then he was kissing her. Their lips just touched, without any planning or anything, and she was kissing him back, very sweetly, gently. Her mouth was so soft and kind of trembly. He could feel her pulse leaping up when his hand touched her throat, just under her chin. It only lasted a minute. They moved away from each other, but only inches away. He could still feel her breath on him, warm and nice. In the light of the low bulb over their heads, her face had a look of happiness that made his heart jump a little bit.

"Good night, Jeff," she whispered, very tenderly.

"Good night."

She moved away from him, and put her hand on the door to open it.

"Lee?"

"Yes?" She half turned around toward him.

"Good night."

She laughed. "Yes, isn't it? A very good night. See you, Jeff."

"See you. . . ."